Susan Hawthorne is an award-winning writer of fiction, non-fiction and poetry. Her works include a novel, *The Falling Woman* (1992), *Limen*, a verse novel (2013) and poetry collections *Lupa and Lamb* (2014), *Cow* (2011), *Earth's Breath* (2009) and *The Butterfly Effect* (2005) among others. She has been the recipient of international residencies in Rome and Chennai, had her work played on ABC's *Poetica* and been included in a number of *Best of* anthologies. She has translated literary works from Sanskrit, Greek and Latin and her books and poems have been translated into Arabic, French, Spanish, German, Chinese and Indonesian. Susan was the winner of the 2017 Penguin Random House Best Achievement in Writing in the Inspire Awards for her work increasing people's awareness about epilepsy and the politics of disability.

Other books by Susan Hawthorne

fiction
Limen (2013, verse novel)
The Falling Woman (1992/2004)

poetry
Lupa and Lamb (2014)
Valence: Considering War through Poetry and Theory (2011, chapbook)
Cow (2011)
Earth's Breath (2009)
Unsettling the Land (with Suzanne Bellamy, 2008, chapbook)
The Butterfly Effect (2005)
Bird and Other Writings on Epilepsy (1999)
The Language in My Tongue (1993)

non-fiction
Bibliodiversity: A Manifesto for Independent Publishing (2014)
Wild Politics: Feminism, Globalisation and Bio/diversity (2002)
The Spinifex Quiz Book (1993)

anthologies
Horse Dreams: The Meaning of Horses in Women's Lives
(with Jan Fook and Renate Klein, 2004)
Cat Tales: The Meaning of Cats in Women's Lives
(with Jan Fook and Renate Klein, 2003)
September 11, 2001: Feminist Perspectives (with Bronwyn Winter, 2002)
Cyberfeminism: Connectivity, Critique and Creativity (with Renate Klein, 1999)
Car Maintenance, Explosives and Love and Other Lesbian Writings
(with Cathie Dunsford and Susan Sayer, 1997)
Australia for Women: Travel and Culture (with Renate Klein, 1994)
Angels of Power and Other Reproductive Creations (with Renate Klein, 1991)
The Exploding Frangipani: Lesbian Writing from Australia and New Zealand
(with Cathie Dunsford, 1990)
Moments of Desire: Sex and Sensuality by Australian Feminist Writers
(with Jenny Pausacker, 1989)
Difference: Writings by Women (1985)

DARK MATTERS

A novel

Susan Hawthorne

First published by Spinifex Press, Australia

Spinifex Press Pty Ltd
PO Box 5270, North Geelong, Victoria 3215
PO Box 105, Mission Beach, Queenslad 4852
Australia

women@spinifexpress.com.au
www.spinifexpress.com.au

Cover image by Suzanne Bellamy
Cover design by Deb Snibson, MAPG
Typeset in Australia by Blue Wren Books
Typeset in Albertina
Printed by McPherson's Printing Group

National Library of Australia Cataloguing-in-Publication

Hawthorne, Susan.
Dark Matters: A novel/ Susan Hawthorne.

ISBN: 9781925581089 (paperback)
ISBN: 9781925581119 (ebook : epub)
ISBN: 9781925581096 (ebook : pdf)
ISBN: 9781925581102 (ebook : kindle)

Subjects: Lesbians–Crimes against–Chile–Fiction.
Violence–Fiction
Homophobia–Chile–Fiction.
Poetry–Psychological aspects–Fiction
Families–Fiction.
Greece–Fiction.
Chile–Fiction.

This project has been assisted by the Australian Government through the Australia Council, its principal arts funding and advisory body.

This novel is inspired by
Consuelo Rivera Fuentes from Chile
Christine from Uganda
X from Australia
and the many undocumented lesbians
who have been tortured, murdered
and their histories erased.

write, write or die.
—H.D., 1960

*The body remembers and pain becomes part
of our dreams and of our nightmares …*
—Consuelo Rivera-Fuentes, 2001

*"Hope" is the thing with feathers —
That perches in the soul —
And sings the tune without words —
And never stops — at all —*
—Emily Dickinson, 1861

Luna runs past me, barking and heads out the door.

José shouts from the gate. "Mercedes. It's me. Can I come in?"

I pull myself up from my chair. He's still standing there when I reach the front door.

"Okay," I say, "come on in."

"Coffee?"

"Yes please, just what I need."

We move out to the deck, each seated so we can catch the breeze and see the view. We look out over the sea. My eagle swoops into view. White-breasted, silent as a stealth fighter. The usually ebullient José is quiet. I wonder why he's travelled a whole day to visit me.

"They've released Kate," he says, without warning, without warming up even.

I say nothing.

José looks at me. I return his gaze. Nothing frightens me any more.

"You know," he says, "she's going to want some explanation, some contact."

"It's too soon." My heart falls. Almost fails. Don't cry, I tell myself. Don't react. I turn my head away.

"I think you owe her, Merci."

"Owe her what?"

"A story."

"Why?"

"You don't know what she's been through."

"No. Do you?"

"Well, no, but yes a little. She doesn't want to talk much. I guess it's too painful just now."

"So why tell me then? Why did she call you? She hasn't asked me, so drop it."

"She's being careful. Surely you know that."

The wind picks up and the trees between the sea and us begin to flutter their leaves. He's looking into the empty coffee glass as if trying to see through the dark dregs at its base.

"Is there anything I can tell Kate?"

"Nope."

"I know you don't want to see her yet …"

"You know I can't afford to see her or anyone else. Remember what happened in Santiago and Concepción? Remember Carmen? She thought it was okay too. Remind Kate of this. Do you get it?"

"Let me finish, Merci. I know you don't want to see her yet, but if you change your mind, if you want me to pass on something, I'll do it. Okay?"

"Hmmn," I breathe out. "Okay."

His knees bend and he rises from the chair with such ease, that I sometimes gasp at how everything in his body works together.

"Can I stay in my usual room," he says. "No need for you to come with me. I know the way blindfolded."

He leaves the room, picks up his backpack and heads across the garden. I sit in my chair watching the sea's horizon, my heart in turmoil.

DESI

Last night watching TV, it occurred to me that Kate's former neighbour, Alma Bocca, might be the filmmaker whose work I found online. If so, at the one time living in this street were three amazing women: Mrs Alma Bocca, filmmaker, Mrs Johanssen, wildlife carer at the zoo and Mrs Gardiner, environmentalist and artist. Could they all have been lesbians? That was in the days before the word Ms was widely used. Back then this was not the fashionable artsy suburb it is now. But the lesbians had already moved in.

That's the thing about lesbians, it's a kind of detective story that unwinds in scraps but half of the pages are shredded and the rest are so destroyed as to be unreadable. What we have left are fragments. This story therefore is told in fragments; those I have been able to piece together. I'm Desi, niece of Kate who sometimes used her birth name Ekaterina when she wanted to be noticed.

My Aunt Kate was a lesbian, and before her, her great aunt. Before that, who knows? Her great aunt, Eudy, went into exile and like so many, hardly left any footprints. Kate, by contrast, left behind a huge swathe of writings, but most of it never made it off her computer, or was published only in fragments, or published in tiny magazines, or published in so many different ways that hardly anyone ever managed to put these fragments together.

Why bother, you ask, who wants to read about a few old dykes, old ducks? You'd be amazed. I was. In fact, I could hardly believe what I was reading half the time. Oh, I forgot to mention how I came across all this stuff. Well, my maiden aunt, that old dyke, left me a whole lot of boxes, a few books and some diaries. And the house. What am I going to do with these? I thought. Out of indecision, I stacked them away in the back room. One day, I was having a big clean up and about to junk the lot. I sat down to read a few of the scraps of paper and was bowled over. Not by all of it, but enough to make me think that I should keep it, at least long enough to sort out what was worth keeping and what was not.

It's been three years since I opened that first box and started reading and I finally know what I want to do. I've enrolled in a degree in creative writing. I said rather lamely in my application that I was looking into the ways in which women passed down memorabilia through their families, in particular looking at women who do not have children. *Diagonal Genealogies,* I called it.

It turns out that the story of Kate and Mercedes is way more interesting than I ever imagined. There's not much from Mercedes, just a few letters. The rest is Kate, though she also writes under the name Ekaterina.

The problem is, and don't tell the examiners, sometimes I don't know if it's me writing, or her? Or them? It's all so weird.

> ancient writing happens in many different ways
> in Crete it resembled their method of ploughing
> called boustrophedon

What the fuck is a boustrophedon? It turns out that it has to do with cows. Kate was obsessed with cows. There are cows here and cows there. These ones are cows from Crete thousands of years ago. They walk in a zigzag (a bit like my inheritance down through the auntie line) long parallel lines that go back and forth across the paddock (she was a farm girl after all). Those old Cretans then turned it into a method of writing.

backandforthacrossthepageinacontinuo
teguoynehwdnaskaerbynatuohtiwworsu
totheotherlineyoujustkeepgoingbackwar
telbaebotevahuoyesuacebhcnubtramssd
oreadbothways

You see what I mean! No simple task. Anyway, this back and forth thing intrigued her I guess. As did moving backwards and forwards in time. She never stayed put. Late twentieth century or five thousand years before now. Reading her is like reading the weather. Sometimes you get it right, often you don't.

Mercedes is forever telling me stories about her ancestors. That's because when her family moved to Melbourne, along with suitcases, they brought the entire family – and not just the current generation, but going back over hundreds of years. She can rattle off ancestry as if it were just one of those seven impossible things you get done before breakfast. Their suitcases rattled with the bones, the hearts, lungs and spleen of bloodlines.

But me, my family left those memories behind in the far off villages of Crete. I get lost going back only a couple of generations. I know their names, but I hardly know who they were. That's one of the losses of migration. My grandmother was one of seven daughters – that was an auspicious beginning. Seven sisters, just like the Pleiades. Here is what I know.

Ally, eldest daughter. They grew up in the mountains in Crete. Ally was as sharp-eyed as a kingfisher. I have a memory of her, sitting beside the open front door sewing gingham dresses for my cousin and me. Red gingham with white cross-stitch for my cousin; blue gingham with white cross-stitch for me. She travelled around Europe in the 1920s. Went to grand-sounding meetings that might have changed the world if the next war hadn't come. When it did, the world changed. So many dead, so many hiding in caves where the Germans could not find them.

Lecca, had a face like the moon, round and bright. I saw her when we travelled to Greece to see all the aunts and uncles, cousins and grandparents. She was old and as frail as a stalk of wheat. She simply lay in that bed, silent. No words, no memories to share with the little girl beside the bed.

The third sister, Maia, was a fine storyteller. Maia, my grandmother. So much to say about her, and yet so little. It's my emotions that rev up at the thought of her. She used to watch the boxing. She lived in Irakleion. I remember her sitting beside me. I had mumps while we were there. She must have told me stories, because that's what I feel I remember. We stayed for a year and then returned to the farm back in Australia. My father returned after just a few months because they couldn't get through the shearing and harvesting without him.

Another was called Tiggy, a reader, quiet as a doe, but behind that shield, a sharp mind. Tiggy, mother of Loukas the artist and boatman, I see her in her tiny kitchen. She's explaining to me why the English word ballet is pronounced –ay– at the end instead of –ett–. In summer Loukas takes us out on his boat, sailing out across the sea, sometimes as far as Santorini's moon bay.

One of the family puzzles is Mari who moved from the mountains down to the sea. Of all the sisters, she's the only one who looks sad most of the time. There's an old-fashioned element to her – her cotton dresses just a bit too long, her face expressing something I can't quite get a grip on. She took up with Giannis, a sailor, who had a great sense of humour. She shared a small house with her sister Callie, whose highjinks must have rubbed off on her. She married Giannis just before we left for Australia.

The youngest and most fun loving was dark-eyed Callie. Callie was my favourite. Her voice still vibrates through my soul. Deep and resonant. In our time in Crete we stayed with Callie and Mari (always in that order) many nights when our parents were away in those first few months – who knows where they went, what they did – for a few days or a week. And we were in heaven. Taken to the beach, where we swam and played. She too married. A Belgian, can't remember his name. He'd spent years in Africa and brought with him treasured art, carved wood for his gallery visited by summer tourists. Were these objects stolen?

From our last summer in Greece, I remember a painting. It must have come from the Belgian. A huge painting of a chook, streaked with colours. This chook must have been a Belgian chicken, sophisticated, elegant, a city chook. Not like the poor old dried out hens we had back home in Australia that panted around the water trough on hot dusty days. Callie's apartment, on the waterfront at Chania, was filled with paintings and artwork from so many places. I wonder now if I'd have liked her after all. I suspect that we'd have been at opposite ends of the political spectrum.

And finally, Aunt Eurydice, she was always disappearing with her girlfriends. Eventually she went so far away, her sisters never saw her again. There are three photos of her. In one she is standing alone. It is such a small photograph I can't see the features of her face. In the second photo, because I don't know her, I cannot pick her out in the one taken with so many of the sisters in Paris in the early 1920s. What were you doing there? Living it up? Finding love or a companion?

The last photo is of Eudy standing on the moors or some other wind-blasted place with another woman. Who is she?

Ruby. You are the mystery woman in the photo with Eurydice. I found your name in a letter which was signed, Eudy and Ruby.

But when we left Crete, I lost them. Lost all six great-aunts and my grandmother at once. Gone were the stories. Gone were the walks into the hills to pick olives. Gone were the afternoons of golden light when I would sit next to Maia and watch her milk the goat. She let me pull at the teats too sometimes. Warm, soft, it made me feel all squeezy inside (that's what I called it). I lost a whole world at a single blow. Each Christmas there would be gifts, but how could they remember what size I was? How could they know what now held my interest? Only the wrapping paper and the cards really sang to me. Every year or so there was one fewer sister, until one year, no gifts came, no cards, no fine wrapping paper.

Language makes us. But we too remake language. And ourselves. If we listen, imagine, invent.

Listen to me. Listen to my language. Once upon a time it was the language of the birds. Did you listen then? Are you listening now?

I'm a person out of place. Perhaps a person without a place. But that cannot be. Surely, everyone has a place? But is the place in this time?

Let me begin again. Once upon a time … it was a very long time ago. More generations than you can count on your hands and your toes. It was in the time when the first stirrings of language were in our throats. A time of gurgling and burbling, of whistling and of singing.

It was the singing that began language. We imitated the birds. And slowly, so very slowly, words began to take shape. Words formed from the electrical charges in our brains. Concepts arising with each new song. And so, in a way, we sang ourselves, our communities into being.

DAY 1

I don't know where I am. They came hooded. Shouting, waving their guns. They were wearing boots and hooded jackets. Inside the hoods their mouths were covered by some kind of wrap. From behind they looked like aliens without necks. The hoods dropping straight to their backs. I heard a shot. A neckless one stood holding my beautiful Priya by one leg, dropped the dog body on the floor as if discarding an old rag. Another shot rang out. As I watched she fell in slow motion to the floor.

I don't know why I'm here. Wherever here is.

They pushed me into a van. I heard another shot as they slammed the van door on me. Mercedes? I was scared, so very scared. No markers. Nothing to tell me what the meaning of this could be. The van sped along the highway for a long time. Three hours maybe. Then we began to take a route that resembled a bowl of spaghetti. Any sense of direction I might have had vanished. Finally we hit a bumpy track, full of pot holes. The side to side swaying shifted to vertical jolting. I was sore by the time we arrived here. Wherever here is. I'm repeating myself. I want to know.

They opened the van door and shoved a heavy cloth over my head. It was still dark but I thought I glimpsed some light on the clouds before the hood covered my eyes. Hands pulled at my arms, hauling me out and pushing me again. I tripped over a step as they led me inside. The first thing that hit me was the smell. It still is. It's the smell of animal urine mixed with fear.

Where was I? Language. Where did it come from? I need to start at the beginning. I need to restart if I lose my place. If I lose my will.

What I see is a group of women sitting on a hill. In the middle is a small fire. Something is cooking. A sweet smell fills my nostrils. It is quiet except for the occasional bird song. A woman taps another on the shoulder and points to where the sound comes from. She purses her lips and a strange air-filled whistling begins. The other women laugh. Mercedes is there among them. Her eyes shining with that dazzling dark light of hers. She touches me.

This imagined place reminds me of so many places I've been. It's a mix of many hills from many countries. But the colours, they are the colours of Australia. The dry places that still suffuse my memory. The light of late afternoon that I've not seen anywhere else. The sun hangs low, hugging the horizon and turns everything gold and shining. There's a particular view from the top of the tank stand at the old farm, looking through the eucalypts towards the dam. My brother and I used to climb up the metal ladder and sit. We'd watch the house cow meander across the paddock. Watch as the sun spread either side of a black callitris trunk, and then turn pink as it hit the flat edge of the world. There's a spot next to Cooper Creek where the sun hangs forever spreading its wattle shower.

I stumbled as they pressed me into a room. They shouted and manhandled me to a wall. Hands up. Legs apart. They placed me so that my hands were above my head. My legs in the military at ease position. But this was not at ease. I felt something hard in my back. A weapon? I shifted just a little. They shouted, prodded me in the back again and moved me back to the original position. I stood. And stood. And stood. The aching began. Fear was spreading through me like a drug. I wanted to think about something else. Imagine myself in a different place. But my brain kept pulling me back to the now. My body ribbed with bars of pain. The body its own kind of prison. My hands were trying to read the wall. The wall blocked from me by the hood. Cold. Stone. A rough surface. Can't tell if it's rock or manmade. It feels thick.

As sight is shut off everything else intensifies. My ears have become antlers. I allow all the sounds to wash over me. Voices. Look at those hairy legs, says one of the two right behind me. Other voices mix further away. Clatter of footsteps. An echo of nothing. Like a hollow space between the ears. *Amo*, my brain starts up. *Amo, amas, amat. Amamus, amatis, amant.* Miss Lupa. Latin. Wolf woman. I only realised that later. *Amo, amas amat, amamus, amatis, amant.* How many times did we repeat that? How was I to know then that it was love that defined her, and would me too. *Bellum, bellum, bellum, belli, bello, bello. Bella, bella bella, bellorum, bellis, bellis.* That's what this is. They've finally done it. Declared war on us.

Mercedes, are you my wolf woman? They would say devil.

I'm a wolf, loping (louping) through the forest. My gait is even and measured. I can do this for hours, days, stopping only to mark my territory. Like the wolf, I am condemned. I am hunted. I cross vast expanses of country only to come face to face with the hunter. My only advantage: I smell him before he sees me. After days of moving, I am hungry. My appetite is me. I sink onto my haunches and wait. I have the patience of a wolf.

I will myself to have patience. To still my hunger. Like the wolf I must wait. Turn the tables and tell myself that it's not me who is the hunted, in the end it is them. They will fall prey. Even if it means that I drown with my wolf self, better that than that I give myself to them. Better that I should drown than betray all that I've lived for.

It's been building over years. With each election new laws were introduced. Laws that pulled most into the system. But as the rest were pulled in, we became more visible. More trouble. And we appeared more radical than ever. Not much had changed, just the contrast made sharper. I hadn't heard that we were in danger. I've always been outspoken. Is that why me?

A burning rod. My body taut with pain. I'm a violin whose strings have been tightened too much. Touch me and I'll howl like discordant strings. A threnody of loss. Strings wailing with grief. Will I break? Will they break me?

They've put on a CD. At first I thought, good, I won't have to listen antennae-eared to their movements, their disparaging comments behind me. But this can't count as music. Banging, barraging sound meant to deafen me and drive me mad. I want ear-plugs. No services on this flight out of reality. The sound burns through me. Now and then I catch a phrase. Hate-filled.

How long have I been here?

Go back. Back to the beginning again. Beginning with what? With O? With zero? With the circle? When did the voices emerge? Was it when the women stuck out their lips and allowed a low sound to roll up from the diaphragm? Or was it the short sharp ooo-ooo sound of a chimpanzee? Or was it the aum rolling up from the back of the mouth, across the palate, onto the lips and out through spacetime? There are so many puzzles to unwind.

I thought the zero had come out of the desert, out of the paradise that was once Mesopotamia, now a rubble of war memorials and ruins. Ruined lives. Where once the women rode wild horses, where hanging gardens were designed by queens not short on ideas, nor on power. These are not even memories any more. The sites have been bombed, the treasures hidden away or blown up. Who wants to keep evidence that women once were not in thrall to men? If George Orwell were around, even he would be shocked at the revisionism, the rewriting of history, the public annihilation of memory, the reversal of truth. Of course, there are many who hold to it in private. And I am one of them.

But there's an earlier zero in Prakrit and Sanskrit texts from India, what's later called shunya in the Brahminic language of Sanskrit.

I'm still standing. My head covered. Waves of dizziness come over me. My legs have turned to steel. Mercedes … is she here too? Who do they have? Who have they rounded up? It's the butterfly effect. Not as physicists imagine it. Although similar. It's just as Monique said. The ritual of the butterfly. Virginia's wall with the mark left by the moth. The mark we leave. Dead or alive. My arms are growing wings. Wings of heavy metal. Collapsing wings. Too heavy like the wings of the Hercules moth, caught on the wall. Drawn to the light. But too frail to fly. I leave my body, pick up the moth and carry her to the railing, hoping that the extra height will help her fly.

Mercedes, Mercedes, Mercedes. Where are you? Are you here too? Did they pick you up during the dawn raid? Tell me you're here. No, please don't let you be here.

Night night night. Dark with fear and pain. The kind of night when you would hear the curlews sing. Whistling up the ghosts of the dead. Could I be dead? In death there's no pain. Here there is pain and more pain. I can hear the scraping of feet on the stone. Stone or brick? Stone, too irregular for brick. My head is heavier than it's ever been. Rock heavy. My neck feeling its weight. Will I crumble? I can't, I can't, I can't. I mustn't.

What was the catalyst? Why have they arrested me? Which article? Which poem? Which speech? Or is it something else? If only I knew what else. But I have to assume that I am alone here. I have to fill my mind with strength. God knows how. What if I'm not strong? I will fill my mind with Mercedes. Imagine her body against mine. Imagine skin and hair, muscle, laughter and warmth. All I can hear now is my breathing. Laboured. Not much more to hear apart from the footsteps that come and go. That and the muscles shaking through the skin.

I haven't slept. Can't sleep standing against the wall. My fingers and toes gave way and they left me. But my steel-rod arms are still above my head. Is there any blood in my fingers? I can't look. But I can't feel either. When I tried to drop my arms they yelled and forced them up again.

Each time I am forced to raise my arms, I imagine that I am some kind of insect with arms like feelers, straight out in front. The insect is my inspiration. I imagine myself doing some incredible acrobatic feat, hanging from one arm, the body rising magically into the air. Sitting on a giant winged motorbike that is soaring through the air. The insect model is playing with my mind. Everything becomes a version of an insect. So many patterns. Dragonfly landing on the surface of a pond making no ripple. Mosquitoes whirring like broken down air-conditioners on a hot night. I can't believe all the things my brain is serving up to me. Where do these obsessions come from?

If we go back again to the women in the ur-place – perhaps it's Mesopotamia or the Indus Valley, perhaps it's a waterhole or creek in the Australian desert, perhaps it's an ash-covered rift valley in Africa – wherever it was, the insects were there too. The women are putting their tongues behind their teeth and imitating bees or mosquitoes or flies. It's the voice again. And the mouth. The original O. Or was it?

DESI

I am in a chaos of papers and boxes and I don't know where I am going. It's like the universe at its beginning. Those few orderly boxes have exploded. There are galaxies and solar systems, stars and moons. On the edge of our solar system are the Oort Clouds. Beyond them our sun has an imaginary twin, Nemesis, her existence hypothetical and although the search continues, she has been declared non-existent. Imperceptibility is not a clue to non-existence, as Vera Rubin discovered. Way way out there somewhere at the edge of things or so close we can't see it is dark matter, that imperceptible region. Getting off track here. What I am facing is a chaotic pile of papers and I have no idea where to start.

I wish Kate had been a Virgo because then I'd have some chance of following her schema.

Movement begins around me. The sound of stumbling steps. Others? Who? Where are they taking them? They pull me from the wall and push me across the room. Released, I almost fall. Someone grabs me. Yanks me over to a wall and leaves me there unaided, standing with my arms hanging lifelessly from my shoulders. Someone comes, lifts my hands and binds them in front of me.

The rough handling ceased. Some other hands took over. Gentler somehow. I was filled with a desire to smile. Such a relief. I wanted to yell out, Thank you. But I didn't. I couldn't. Not until I knew what was happening. The gentle hands led me along what sounded like a corridor. There were echoes. We turned and turned again, then stopped at a door. Gentled inside to a bed, they made it impossible for me to stand, and so I sat. Then they left. Not a word.

Where am I? I've lost the plot. My inside story is smashed to pieces and I am going to have to start all over again. You can't think in the midst of panic. All that happens is that the autonomic system takes over. It overrides everything else. The mind retreats in a body panic. All the stories you've told yourself to stay calm. All the stories that have enabled you to lift out of this animal house recoil, disappear into another realm. Almost anywhere will do.

I sat. And sat. A great blank fear inside me. Not like the earlier panic. Somehow worse. I stood. It took me ages to stand. My hands, bound in front of me, were not tight, but I could not feel around me as you would when blinded. I moved like a snail so I wouldn't injure myself. Was there a low ceiling? A ledge? A barrier? I could stand full height. There are some advantages to being short. Then I began the shuffle. Snail-like again. Well, really more like a slug as I had no shell to protect me. I moved small creep by small creep, exploring the space with my feet. It was uneven. Maybe stone. I found the walls and brushing the wall with my body felt the texture. Cold and rough. A ledge or the promise of a high window I found on the third wall. As I shuffled toward the last wall, there was a clang. It startled me. I lifted my right foot and felt the outline. A bucket? I gave it a nudge. Yes, a bucket.

After what I've started to call 'the struggle' I was half sitting on the bucket, pissing into it. Then 'the reverse struggle' while I moved back toward the bed. At least I now knew the geography of the room. I lay down and slept.

the deathless ones live beyond our paltry deaths
we will perish before their endless lives

Heraclitus, Fragment 67

What is worse, to live endlessly through pain? Or to die because some guard is having a bad day? How paltry is such a death? Is it perhaps clever to get out while the going is good? How good can eternal life be? And if it is so good, why is it that the gods don't seem to get any smarter with all that age?

My head is oceanic. Full of tides and undercurrents. An eddying ocean. Skylla and Charybdis whirling round one another like lovers dancing the tango. A ceaseless flow, this way and that. The cows are coming, fifty head of them pounding across the ocean. Making waves. Was it FannyAnn who was murdered? Was she trampled? And who was it that decided it was time for her to go? For nine nights, the nine daughters of Memory cradled her in their arms. Mother Memory where are you? In this darkest place of all, who will help me? What will this dark night bring? Oh Nemesis be mine!

DESI

Something strange is going on here – is she having a religious phase? This one has Ekaterina written in Greek at the top. Why is she in prison? I don't know about these prisons. Although during the time she was writing this there was an escalation of prison building. Boat people incarcerated as if they were criminals, not people fleeing for their lives. And even the wildlife parks were affected. They started to build high-walled green fences for captive breeding programs of our native animals. The locals protested, but nobody could prove anything. Just a whole lot of greenwashing. That was before there was a surge in new criminal offences.

This fragment was in a different box from the prison stories. It was difficult with the prison stories to know the precise order. The pages are collected in different bundles, sometimes with the Day number written, sometimes not, so I've tried to keep those bundles together.

DAY 2

I wake to the sound of carolling magpies and the early morning cough of wattle birds. For a moment I am free, and then the memory of yesterday shatters me awake. I feel pain in my hips and around my waist. My arms still feel like lead, and with every movement I make my muscles scream. I lie, breathing through the cloth that covers my head. The sound of birds is amplified. I had hoped that in the light this head covering would be more transparent. It chokes me in darkness. Without the birds I could not know the time of day. I listen to their song. Try to pull it into my heart, filling myself with its memory.

Memory. And I am overcome by your scent, your very particular smell. Like a mix of spices, but none of them have names.

What was it I was telling myself? Stories. About the invention of language. About the women who invented not only language, but the zero, and the wheel, and the Hanging Gardens of Babylon with its complicated system of watering. A bad idea. It gave people the idea that we had power over nature. But who are we to think we can do any better than the dinosaurs?

But language, now that was a good idea. And with language came storytelling, with storytelling came dance and probably art. Our imaginations reaching for the stars and sometimes incorporating them into our story legends. The stars became communities of people who had been here before, or were about to visit, or were in exile for some crime. They were wordless but we women were not.

We fossicked for food and told stories about what we found and where we found it. We sniffed, and tasted only when our guts told us it was safe. We carried foodstuffs back to camp and shared it, so we each tasted one another's find.

Here I am thinking about food again.

DESI

I've started to find some of the poems she's written. There is a series (maybe incomplete or perhaps I just haven't found them all yet) of poems to the Muses. The first I came across was about dancing.

dance dance dance
dance the trata in your
red white and black garb
dive down dive down
dive underground

    dance dance dance
    dance the trata
    for bread and pomegranate

      dance as we have
      for millennia
      as is carved
      on the tomb
      of the dancing women

        dance a zigzag
        dance the weave of a basket
        dance the stars and spirals
          inwards
          outwards

        enter the labyrinth
        with the young ones leading
        dance as if your life depends
        on the dance

          sing with the old ones
          sing out your strong voices
          voices that hold the world
          sing like swallows
          twittering to bring spring

            dance dance dance
            sing sing sing
            dance the trata
            sing the spring

DAY 2

My legs are free and I lift my bare feet into the air, exploring the
space around the bed like a Kafkaesque insect caught on its back.
Not much. A bare wall made of brick or smooth stone. It is cold
in the morning air. I sit up, pulling to vertical with my stomach
muscles. My hands, still tied in front of me are not very helpful.
This slow entry into the morning is broken by shouting. My heart
jump starts and my aerial ears are receivers. The shouting rises
and then retreats. I breathe out and stand. I move in the direction
of the bucket, my foot recognising its metallic feel. I want this
over and done with before they come shouting in at me.

If I were an athlete would it help? Would it mean that I could
break out of here? Would it mean that I could climb the walls, a
Chinese acrobat hanging on with spider feet? Like the trapeze
artist who escaped from Ravensbrück. They keep on at me. They
ask questions I cannot answer. Yesterday they threw words at
me, trying to unsettle me. Slut, they said. Gypsy. Whore. Scum.
Moll. Sexpot. Scavenger. Ho. Nympho. Hooker. Cunt. Slack-arse.
Fucking pro. I kept my silence. I did not deny. Nor did I agree.

In my hooded darkness, I thought I saw Priya. In the shadows
of my cell. She was curled in the corner, waiting. I tried to stand
up and whispered her name, Priya. But she was gone. Mercedes,
Priya is here, where are you?

It was Ochi Day and I was travelling in the mountains in Crete. I hadn't remembered the story of Ochi Day. It was the day the Greeks celebrated saying no, ochi or οχι to Mussolini. That no, meant that Greece would be attacked as they were on 28 October 1940.

I was on the Lasithi Plateau in the village of Psychro chasing archaeological sites. It was cold so I went to bed early and woke to the sound of such loud music I had to get up and see what was happening. A building some distance from my room, a hall filled with people. Women were flinging their arms and legs about in wild dancing. I sat for a while, not wanting to intrude but as the music wound up even more I had to dance. The walls spun, the music welled, faces and bodies in movement. The people around smiled at me, a woman grabbed my hand and led me across the dance floor and back again several times, and as she let go she sent me spinning. I sat down again and caught my breath.

The next day I headed for the Diktaian Cave. It's the cave where Zeus brought Europa when he abducted her. Zeus transformed himself into a white bull. Europa like all ancient girls was out picking flowers with her friends. She patted him and being an adventurous young woman, climbed up to ride on his back. Bad mistake because Zeus took off, swam towards Crete and brought her to Diktaian Cave. It was her line from which all the Minoans were descended.

There wasn't much to see outside the gate to the cave. The tourist season was finished and the gate was closed. I climbed the fence and entered through a narrow cleft as you'd expect from an old site sacred to the mother of Crete. It opened out into several 'rooms', some with beautiful stalactites. I paused, feeling my heart expanding. Not one for acts of reverence, I was surprised to find my hand touching my forehead then my heart. The darkness enclosed me. So rare, but a feeling of immense safety swept over me. I took tentative steps into the deeper darkness, my hands tracing the lumps of wall as I moved slowly down. I have no idea how long I walked and sat and listened. It might have been years. As I turned to retrace my steps, tears – like the drops of water in a cave – were running down my face. I paused again in the first circle of light. I headed back, up the now bright path into blinding light. I scrabbled over the fence hoping no one would see me and returned to town for a sweet coffee.

DAY 2

The door opens. Footsteps come towards me. They pull at the hood. It's too tight to come off. They undo the string and air rushes across my face. He turns and all I see is a retreating head and neck in the flare of sudden light. I sit and stare while my eyes adjust. It's half-light. I'm looking at the walls, at the position of the bed in relation to the ledge, at the location of the bucket. Near the door there's a cardboard tray. I stand slowly and walk over. Look down to see a plastic cup with some brown liquid in it. A bread roll and a tin of Spam. When I look at this I'm not hungry, although my insides are gnawing. It must be twenty-four hours since I've eaten. I pick up the bread. It's stale and hard. I try the liquid. Cold dishwater, cheap instant coffee. I leave the slices of tinned meat. I tuck it up behind the ledge. Maybe if I get hungry enough I'll be able to eat it. Or maybe some animal will come to share the space.

Ironic to be accused of selling sex. Is that what they want of us? Is that what they think we long to do? It's their idea of living, not mine. That place was so seedy. Where the men came to take photographs. All the girls were barely out of school. Too naïve to understand that the money was not worth the indignity. There I stood in my yellow underpants which on that day seemed to barely cover me. I was not especially thin, I had puppy fat. But I had the requisite long hair. I tried for the look. I'd never seen a photographer's studio before. He had a silver umbrella for dispersing the light. For him it was just business. These days I wonder what happened next. What happened with those photos? Do they circulate somewhere as pornographic spam that come to me and millions of others daily? His photos went into The Book. It contained a gallery of girls, and work depended on what the men saw in them. They came with their instamatics and their SLRs and occasionally a Hasselblad. I saw each man only once.

DESI

There are letters too. It's a giant jigsaw and I don't know what the picture on the box should look like. That happened to me once. I'd been hospitalised because my family thought I was nuts. I wasn't, I was just overwhelmed by life and had too many things going on in my head. A friend came to see me. Mostly, my friends just gave up on me. Loony bin, I could hear them say in their neat school uniforms. But this one came. She was a bit stuck for words. I don't blame her, nut houses have that effect on even the most hardened souls. She brought me a jigsaw. Every afternoon I sat on the floor and tried to put the pieces together. It wasn't until I was some way into it that I realised the picture on the box wasn't the same as the picture on the jigsaw. And I'd tried so hard to make it fit.

But that friend with her wonky present really helped me. I couldn't fit the picture, no matter how hard I tried. And my family, well, they were playing with a completely different set of pictures from mine. Their pictures were of tame parks with ordered beds and flowers all in a row. Mine? It was a moisture-filled rainforest and the smell of rotting fruit. Through the trees would come the call of birds, the scuttle of lizards in under-growth, and the quiet wilting of fungi.

Not much rainforest here in the city, but out the back of my place surrounded by former industrial warehouses I've created a small garden. The plants struggle for want of enough sunlight, like my writing, it's a work in progress.

I was wandering along the matrimonial section of Sydney Road yesterday. It's a wasteland of marriage and divorce. Why would anyone want to gear up and spend all that money? I peered into the shops at bridal gowns and tuxedos, specialist shops for cakes and cards and all that paraphernalia. Even the lesbians are doing it. I want to yell out, do something useful, a relationship is more than one big day, no matter how symbolic it's become.

Querida Mercedes,

I want to tell you about a dream. I am a bird. A bright little sunbird, yellow-breasted. I'm a thrill seeker, hanging from the huge flowers of the heliconia. I dip my beak into the water-filled cup as the sun rises. I see you on the horizon, gliding along the cliff edge. You sweep along with such pace. Meanwhile, in my light-filled tiny body, I am untouched by your hunt for prey. That is, until the day when the earth falls apart, trees bend and snap. The flowers are shredded. There is no food left for any of us. As that day sweeps into being, you appear again on the horizon, but this time you're not flying parallel to the coast, you are flying straight at me. You are silent, a bulwark, both graceful and threatening and then you dive.

I scream at your approach. I cry out, *Mercedes, Mercedes. It's me. Stop. It's me.* But you come straight for me, swoop, and your talons grasp me, lifting me into unconsciousness.

There's a song doing the rounds of my head. It's been there for days and I still can't place it. I know only fragments of lines.

... clouds above the sea ...
the mirror broken ...
sails ... birds on a wing

I know how Sappho must have felt. Broken words. Shards of language. A song fallen apart. I want to sing it to someone. To sing and let my voice ring out. But not here. Give them nothing. Not even a broken song.

The songs. Those hymns. Elegiac and evocative. I'm talking about the Homeric Hymns. O Demeter, you who laughed at the bawdiness of Baubo. Where has our humour gone? Why has the world gone so mad? Was it as mad in your time as in ours? What am I doing here? What do they want of me? Is there anything I can do but sing ancient songs in my head to long dead goddesses?

DESI

Those goddesses are not dead. I mean not dead dead! Not really dead! They keep coming back in cycles. It all depends on who you talk to. I used to have this fuck buddy. He was okay, you know. Just friends really. It started when we were about fifteen. He'd come over and stay. The first night he was so nervous. He slept outside the sheets and so far over that he almost fell out of bed. Mum and Dad thought he was okay, they knew he'd slept outside the sheets – and anyway, better that you know where your daughter is – that was their view. After a while it all went a bit further, it was slow and pretty okay. We spent more time talking than fucking around. We talked about everything: how to get rid of food scraps so they didn't stink (we were green before it was fashionable); how to do yourself in if you needed to; we talked about parallel universes and we agreed that they must exist (I was pretty good on the science of it at the time); we talked of god (no capitals please) and why there weren't any goddesses; we looked at every crack in our bodies; and way more.

There's a gap in the days. Days 3 and 4 are missing. A lacuna as Wittig would say. There are always gaps.

DAY 5

The smell that hit my nostrils on the first night. It still hangs in the air but I'm getting used to it. It's the smell of an abattoir or of a place where animals are slaughtered. Is that what they plan to do to us? I say us, but I don't know who the us is. Only that I can hear others and I'm hoping that I'm not alone. But neither do I wish this on anyone else.

Some days through the smell come other smells. It reminds me of burning flesh. Whose flesh? Animal or human? Mineral, says the clown. Is this a game of twenty questions? It's certainly a game of questions. Like a TV quiz that's gone haywire. Questions that don't make sense. Questions without answers. And the contestants don't know who they're competing against or what they might win. Or lose. Quizland purgatory.

I have been panicking that I will have a seizure and I won't even know that is what's happened. I have no pills here and am surprised it hasn't happened yet. I remember those times when I'd wake in the night and know I had forgotten to carry them with me. One time, a friend raided her mother's valium store. I was in a frantic state doing a cold turkey withdrawal. This is the longest time I've ever gone without my anti-convulsants.

There are things in my head. I'm not sure I'd call them songs yet. But lines half forming and taking me away from this stinking animal stall. This slaughter house.

> Sing to me, oh Muse, of Medea, the woman who has
> travelled far and known much (possibly too much).
> Sing to me, Muse, of days long gone by,
> of times when the world was innocent of modern wrongs.
> Tell me her story: the one who left a land
>
> that might one day have been hers,
> who carried off the sacred symbol, in right
> her own to take. Tell me of the woman who sailed
> away along rivers in unknown countries
> and rough seas, that took her to places where
>
> her law was ignored. Tell me again, oh Muse of poetry
> and song, of the woman who killed to save the world,
> of the woman who returned to the stars
> in a chariot drawn by fiery dragons.
> Nowadays, they say she never existed,
>
> but you and I know better.
> Goddess, daughter of the one that has always
> existed, tell us your tale.

This poem has been banging through my head all night. Building line by line in the style of the Homeric Hymns. My Homeric poem of revenge. If only it were so easy. At least Medea realised before they exiled her that she had been duped. She had been robbed of her land, her dignity, all that was meaningful in her life. So she took her revenge. She killed those whom Jason valued most. Her sons. Her sons who would no longer be hers if he married Glauke. Her sons who would carry on Jason's line, not hers. Would we ever have heard of Medea if she had accepted her lot? What can a woman do when confronted with violations of her dignity, violence against her body? Is there a difference between what men can do and what women can do? The men here – and so far they are all men – their actions are sanctioned by the powerful. The corporations turned governments. What can I do? Write revenge poetry in my head when my sanity allows it?

DAY 5

The food they bring does not come often. It's not the only food here. I can smell the meat they cook for themselves. A barbecue.

When they cook meat I hear noises. Scurrying. Rats? Or is it the bandicoot I have seen on a few occasions? Whatever it is, it likes meat. Even I could eat meat on the days when I smell it. What I get is a thin soupy thing – it is probably meat too but so boiled down there's only the leftovers of bone marrow. A few dead grains float limply through the soup, unrecognisable. The only vegetables that appear in it are the ones I don't like – broccoli, cauliflower, cabbage, brussel sprouts and parsnips. How do they know my dislikes so well?

All this thinking of food is distracting me from my story. I'm not getting very far with it. Perhaps I should start with something easier. Like my life. It's not been a very extraordinary life, but I have to make my brain focus on anything but these dismal surroundings.

I'm fifty-three. For years and years I've been trying to get down on paper my philosophy of life, but never really had the time. Now I have nothing but time. And only my brain to record it.

I'm an optimist. You have to be if you're a feminist in these times. I grew up surrounded by animals and trees and wide open spaces. My childhood was spent out of doors. On the farm.

When my father, Nick, returned home from the war with his new wife, they went back to his childhood farm. The locals took time to discover just how knowledgeable his new Greek wife, Cassandra, was. She knew about farming and was soon a registered wool classer. Also well-versed in the classics. It was tough on her, but she stuck out the hardships. We thought everyone was like us.

After she died, I discovered that she'd had a friendship with the woman who ran the milk bar frequented by the town's miners. Back then, Greeks ran just about every cafe and milk bar in the country, spreading out along the railway lines well away from the cities. I remember sitting in the kitchen behind the milk bar, my mother, whom everyonce called Cass, and Despina drinking sweet Greek coffee, speaking Greek, exchanging news which came from the newspaper, *Neos Kosmos*, distributed along those same railway networks. This was not a public friendship, but they clearly had great fondness for one another. My mother missed her language, her culture, the news of political earth-quakes in faraway Greece.

On the farm, we ran wild, my brother and I. We climbed trees. We spent whole afternoons sitting on the roof of the house, looking out across the hedge and across the flat plains that surrounded the oasis that was our farm. When we weren't on the roof we were pedalling our bicycles as fast as they'd go and doing broadsides on the gravel driveway. We'd have gravel rash at the end of the day. It was a childhood that thrived on physicality. Most days we were swinging from trees, dangling from the bars in the woolshed or in the wheat bin. I guess that's what took me into circus and performance. Having spent my first twelve years hanging by my arms or my legs, it wasn't very scary to get on a trapeze at age twenty-two.

When I joined it was for fun. I just wanted to continue hanging about and learning to do the things I'd seen them do in the travelling circuses that came through our small town about once a year. I remember sitting in the bleachers and watching as the Wirth's aerialists swung and spun and defied gravity. We began because we had something to prove, to ourselves more than anything else. And we learnt so much, about what was possible for each of us, about what scared us and what didn't.

On my first day, there was what Gerry called a fear test. She said, "Okay women, let's see what freaks us out." First up, was a spring board, a gap, and then a crash mat. We had to get across the gap in the most daring way we could. Some leapt with legs running through the air. Fran did the most amazing swallow dive and landed with barely a splash or crash. I decided I could manage a dive roll. Then Gerry pushed the trapeze so that it swung, and this time we had to use the spring board to jump and grab the bar as it swung. It gave me such delight and I smiled as I sprang from the bar onto the other side. Only the wobbly high beam threw me. Turning out there in the middle of the room, a slight wobble in the beam had me shaking, making it worse.

DESI

The good thing about my fuck buddy, his name was Ken, was that we both hated sport. Whenever our families decided to go sporty, get into fitness, even go to a footy match, we'd stick together and think of things we just HAD to do. Net surfing – we called it homework of course – decoding stuff, playing with new programs, calculating the age of the universe. It didn't matter what we said so long as it sounded dumb or smart or something! I have to say why I'm saying 'was' and 'used to' for Ken. He didn't make it. We drifted apart – you know life does that to you. He didn't have another girlfriend because he wasn't into girls – we even talked about it. He did it – and I did it, but it was because everyone expected us to – including our parents. I think all four of them were relieved that we were an item, even if a shaky kind of item. It made *them* feel normal. It worked for us because no one hassled us. They all thought we were long term. After we drifted, he went his own way. Started hanging out in those all-night clubs, fucking in the loos, getting wrecked. Meanwhile I was chilling out in a freezer. Doing nothing except jigsaws without pictures, playing patience, watching gross DVDs, walking and swaying to my internal rhythms. And I slept.

DAY 6

Today was different. There was the usual morning clanging. Voices. The voices behave as though this place is empty. They behave toward me as if I don't exist. They would rather I didn't. How many hoods, how many tightened blindfolds, how many bridal veils or burqas does it take to turn a woman into an object?

They came in early. Shouting as usual. They brought the hood. When I see the hood fear floods me. They always have something up their sleeve. They pushed it over my head. I don't resist. I keep my strength for resisting the things I can do something about. Like my mental state. My breathing. Hands under my armpits, my feet barely touched the floor as they led me along the corridors.

This was a different room. It smelled different. It felt different under my feet. Even the echoes were different. I had a sense of walls that reached higher than the animal stall they keep me in. They stopped next to something flat. Pressed me down. Took my hands and strapped me to the … I cannot call it a bed. They left me there.

I walk through the bush with Cassie. She runs ahead with her ears pricked, every hair on her body alert with anticipation. There are rabbits here. She and I both know this. When we come to an empty warren she sniffs at each burrow, her tail wagging at the vertical, head down, bum up. It takes a while for her to get all the way round the warren. To satisfy herself that the rabbits have moved on.

We head on up the hill, climbing the lichen-covered rocks, taking the direct short route to the top. We are headed for the trig point. From there you can see for miles. The blue-green leaves bend down the hill, pocked by rocky outcrops. On a day like today, the sun warms my back as we sit on the topmost rock. The air is clear and even Old Baldy is visible today.

We sit and Cassie nuzzles up to me, leaning into my side as if her life depended on it.

We take the easy way down, kicking up red dust. Wildflowers dot the edge of the path and I pick a few for Mum. Purple and yellow. Not much leaf on these, but the flowers are profuse. I tickle Cassie behind the ear with the flowers and she bounds off suddenly after the first rabbit of the day.

When I took you there you struggled to understand my emotion. The dry hard soil, the scraggly pines, even the kind of heat. I said, but don't you feel that way. *No*, you said so coldly. I almost shivered in the heat. It took time for me to understand you. We've both come a long way, Mercedes.

DAY 6

They returned making jokes. Speaking about me as if I could not understand them. I understand them far too well. So you think you're better than us? You think that we don't know about you. About your filthy habits. So we're going to help you. Help you rehabilitate. Help you to fulfil your destiny. Help you to become a woman. A real woman. You know what a real woman needs. She needs a real man.

They pulled the hood back and the light almost blinded me. I shut my eyes. Too good even to look at us. They moved in. I don't know how many were in the room. It seemed like masses. They filled the screen of my vision. The 'bed' was low. They approached me with their waistlines above the level of my body. They made me notice their excitement. Not only that, but they used me as a spittoon. They seemed somehow proud of themselves. Now you know just what real men we are. Next time we'll see whether you can be a real woman.

Aaaagh. I vomit. I shake.

I shake and I sprout feathers. I take off and soar: a wedge-tailed eagle. I leave this horror behind.

They left again. The whole group. The door closed and I grapple for something of me, something to keep me whole. There I am, still strapped in, covered by their hate. I cry and cry. Where do all these tears come from? How many tears does it take to wash away my disgust?

I cry. I cry for all. For all the women. For all the lesbians. I cry because no one cries for us. In Kampala and Chicago. We are shot and raped. We are thrown from the top floor of a high building in Tehran and Mecca. When they arrest us, they put us in cells with violent men who think nothing of having their own 'fun'. In Melbourne and on the Gold Coast, we are tossed from cars, rolled into a ditch. In Santiago we are imprisoned and put on the *parrilla*. In Buenos Aires they insist we accompany them to dinner outside the prison. We are caught, used and banged away again at midnight. On the Western Cape they come for so many of us that even the media notices. But most of us remain hidden. There are few reports of the crimes against us. Fewer readers.

DESI

I went dancing last night. I arrived at midnight. The place was abuzz, music blaring, lights pulsating. I sat in the corner and watched. I meant to talk but it was too loud. Anna pulled me up on the dance floor. She was going crazy, leaping about like an emu, all legs. I jigged around thinking about all the papers lying in piles at home and wondering what was in them. I have to read them to sort them. Then Anna was holding me, kissing me and oh, it was all too late to think about filing and sorting.

This morning I was back at it. Synchronicity brought me a new poem that seems to go with the other dance poem about the Muses. It looks as though originally there were twenty poems but usually only nine Muses. Even that old fart, Plato called Sappho the Tenth Muse.

your most recent poems
still make the headlines Psappha
we cite you we remember your lines
and as you'd hoped
someone in some future time
will remember me

we lesbians never believed
the rumours of suicide
from the Leucadian cliffs
we now know that *old age*
has taken its pleasure
turning my black hair white

your ten thousand poems
are fragments shards
of their former selves
your history like so many
to be read in the gaps
in the spaces between the lines

I first read you as lines of graffiti
in the smallest room where
someone wrote *the most beautiful*
thing on this black earth is
whomever you love
for you it was Anaktoria

as the moon rises and sets
I think of you yet again
like so many poets
even more lesbians
whose hearts you
awakened and thrilled

Is any woman real? Since we stopped being queens, since the world is no longer made in our image, none of us is real. Real is what we see before us. What is confirmed by others. What is confirmed by the social order as authentic. How many women have to be killed before men's violence is seen as real? How many women have to be injured and violated before their pain is verified? How many lesbians have to be tortured before our pain is made public?

She teases him and so he murders her. But the court calls it manslaughter. Who here is real? Whose word is truth? She laughs and he kills. She grows strong and he kills. She leaves him and he kills. She takes her children and he kills them all. No wonder we are all going mad with the disconnect between what we know to be true and what is called reality.

Am I mad? Was I mad to say those things about the Party? Should I have held my tongue? But what lesbian can hold her tongue? I shouldn't be making jokes. This is serious. Should I have stilled my pen? Is this what the poets have called writing with your own blood?

How many have they imprisoned? I hear voices but I've seen no one in these corridors. I've not seen a single woman. And yet I feel that there are others here. Is Mercedes here? I wish I knew. Send me a signal, a smoke signal. Anything. Why can't I see your face clearly? Has something happened to you?

DESI

I thought I knew my Aunt Kate. At least better than the others. And she returned the favour a few times inviting me to stay when I came to the city. I thought I knew her because I'd read a few of the things she'd written. I heard some family stories, but when it comes to what made her tick none of them really got it. I still don't know if I do. She was more complicated than she seemed on the surface. You thought she was talking about the things that mattered, and sometimes that was true, but there was another whole underground of knowledge that was shared with her lovers, her friends, her age cohorts, her political allies, perhaps even her rivals.

How do people with a history that is never recognised record it and keep it going? Think of it like this. There's a literature – some of it going back thousands of years, much of it hidden, but brought out, rediscovered every few generations. There's archaeology and architecture, there's art and music, mathematics and science, history and politics – but only a few put it together. Almost no one wants to talk about it. We know there are different worlds in the heads of people from different places. The Indians calculate differently. It makes them look like they have brains like computers. It's simple if you understand Vedic maths. The lesbians (are they a culture?) think differently a lot of the time. It comes from the times they don't spend in straight families. A whole lot of experiences most people take for granted aren't in their lives. Well, not the ones I'm thinking about. No veils, not too many babies or grandchildren (and no contraception). No husbands (a few from the past), and in-laws who would rather they stay away from family occasions (until marriage became the latest fad). What they have is strong back coffees in the late afternoon sun along Brunswick Street. Journeys to weird and wonderful places. Solitude. Conversation – and yet more conversation. Music and art and theatre. And of course, affairs of the heart. Out of this, they bend reality in interesting ways.

A few months after meeting Mercedes, I told her some more about my solo travels in Greece. I said, "Let me tell you a story that I've never told. Will you believe me?"

Once, many years ago I was travelling alone in Greece. I was in the mountains, the mountains of Crete. A place that started with Ana – all the places starting with Ana are high in the mountains. I was walking through a village. All the women wore headscarves of black. They were beautifully embroidered with long tassels hanging from the scarf's edge. I bought one and tied it tightly across my forehead. With it I felt safer. As I walked along a dirt street, I saw a woman standing just outside her front door on a balcony. She stared at me and then after a pause beckoned to me. "*Ela*, come," she said. I was puzzled but also curious, so I went in. I climbed the steps onto the balcony and she invited me into her small kitchen. White walls, Mediterranean blue ceiling, and a blue table in the centre of the room. On the walls were small gold icons. Later, when I looked more closely, I noticed that they all depicted Mary.

She served me a strong cup of sweetened coffee. We exchanged names. Elena she said. When I said Ekaterina, she beamed and said something far too quickly for me to catch. But I heard the word Hekate. After coffee we sat. Me stumbling through some sentences of badly remembered Greek, she patting me on the knee as she responded with more complex ones. I didn't understand it all. So I was a bit surprised when the knee patting turned to hand caressing. She picked up my left hand and pointed to its ringless fingers. Only then did I notice that her hands too were bare. It hit me like an electric jolt. Here was this woman, say in her mid-thirties, too old for the ringless hands to be innocent, who had picked me up, the dykey looking tourist for some sexual gratification. I couldn't decide what to do. On the one hand, I was excited to discover that even in this mountain village there was at least one lesbian. On the other, I wasn't sure that I was ready for a sexual encounter at 11 a.m.

I said, "Psappha," pronouncing it the Greek way. She nodded the Greek way and said, "*Kai mou*," and me, I said leaving her in no doubt that I too was a descendant of Psappha.

There was a moment of silence. Then she grasped my right hand in her two and pulled me towards her. Confusion. My language was not sufficient to go into the subtleties of why I felt myself pulling away. If I walked out then, I would give up the chance of getting to know this woman, of finding a lesbian way into the Greek language and culture. I went with her, discomforted by the dual sense of me using her and she using me.

We were careful. The disrobing was slow and gentle. She gazed at my belly with a sense of admiration. I admired the strength of her arms, the solidity of her hands rough from physical labour. A woman on her own, a lesbian in a Greek village, would have to do everything by herself. We smiled uncertainly as we went down on the cot, for this narrow space could not be called a bed.

Her passion was raw and yet somehow dignified. I felt like an amateur in her arms. As we made love I recalled the images I had seen that morning. The sun in a clear sky, the ragged mountains, the bleating of sheep and goats, and this woman on her balcony. It seemed unbelievable that I should be here in her house.

It wasn't just a one-day stand. I stayed for a while. I was aware of the stares from the village people. It was clear that I was not the first woman to be enticed into this wayward woman's house. We shared our resources. My budget helped her budget and we could even afford a few luxuries. Staying with her helped me too. I had a roof over my head and, in spite of the crush, a kind of bed to sleep in. And my Greek improved by a mile.

Three weeks was long enough. By then we had exhausted our common interests. I could not engage in long conversation, in spite of my childhood language memories returning, my vocabulary was much too juvenile. And I wanted more too. I wanted a woman who really knew something of her Greek lesbian heritage. I had expected her to know things about Crete that her village life had not given her. I told her that she should get out of this village, move to Irakleion or Chania so she could meet others like her. But she was rooted in her village, in a way I could not (and would not) understand. I thought, if I can leave remote rural Australia, why can't you leave isolated village life in Crete? It's a conundrum that exercises me still. How should a lesbian live? Should she prefer the diaspora and lose her roots, or should she remain inside an oppressive culture and take what comes. Elena had decided to take what comes. And I was one of those who came, and who left just like all the others.

DAY 9

It was a long time before I moved again. Maybe I slept. Maybe I blacked out. Maybe I had a seizure. I don't know. I've had nights of alternating wakefulness and oblivion. I wake in the cold of the night, my arms wrapped around myself. Who else will hold me?

As I lay on that 'bed', I imagined myself in flight. I thought of all those fledglings taking their first flight, their wings and feathers ready to go, but what remains is the courage to stretch out and fly. Throw themselves into the air, to the next branch, or off the cliff face. And so I did. I threw myself into the ether, away from that grubby cell where the men defiled me and themselves. I took flight and did not, could not, look back.

It was like my first day of aerials, grabbing the bar, swinging my legs, making it but awkwardly. No grace, but plenty of determination. It's like that every time I learn a new trick, especially the drops. That moment before the fall. The moment of weightlessness. Drops are weight in downward motion. Flight is weight in upward motion.

Over the tongues of women come honeyed words. While their words are sweet the liquor is strong and they forget what they have said. There are nine daughters of memory and nine of forgetting. At the end of nine days and nine nights the universe comes into being. At least that's pretty much what some of the ancients thought. Nine mothers, nine matrices each carrying a string bag wandering through timespace.

I am awake again. I have developed a small time-filling entertainment for myself. I look into the darkness. And this space is always dark. Darker than the world outside. I raise my hand, usually it's the right hand. And as I raise it slowly above me I watch the shape of the energy through my fingers. It pullulates, a shimmering matrix in the shape of my hand: the palm with its five spokes. Then I raise my left hand. Watch it move through the same series of shapes. Once both matrices are established, I bring my hands together and watch as the two streams seek one another out as they might in prayer.

In the dark I try to see your face. I concentrate on that wisp of hair that always sticks out at an odd angle. The herds are coming with a thundering roar of hooves, like a wildebeest migration. The universe-creating cow is on a journey to visit her long-lost friend, the dark emu, hard to find in the spaces between the darkness. But she persists, dances out through the Milky Way leaving a trail of stars. Shadowing that dark emu in the sky, she picks up pace. Her tail is a long-haired comet, a whiplash in darker regions. The emu comes for me, her vast mouth opens into an abyss of nothingness. I see your eyes and your mouth capable of so many shapes. Emu washes over me filled with dark energies, she pushes through and emerges simultaneously changed and unchanged, as is the way of singularities.

the scope of Psyche can never
be reached though you travel
to its reportedly great depths

Heraclitus, Fragment 71

Psyche is always out of reach. Even the brash Apollo knew that. Seeing her only in the dark, how could he ever be sure what he saw? How bright is the moon when down?

In the dark of a moonless night, how long is a night? How long forever?

I dream in Greek like my grandmother before me. She is telling stories in the old language of Classical Greece. She has waited these fifty years to speak so that I might understand.

How long is forever? Can death be measured?

The soul of Psyche is as deep as moonshine in a bottomless well. My grandmother speaks to me of lost languages.

DESI

I found this fragment of Heraclitus and the musings among her papers. This one has her Greek name, Ekaterina (Εκατερίνα), at the top. She has a real thing about fragments. From Heraclitus, from Sappho, from Woolf and Wittig and HD. (I'd change my name to HD too, if my first name were Hilda and my second Doolittle). They are strewn like markers through her writing. Scraps of paper with phrases on them, like flags.

And then there are the musings on ancestors. On these she has scrawled Kate. She is like a Chinese hagiographer, genealogies of memory. Some are not very accurate in their facts, but she's tried to fill in the emotional genealogy. Cass, too, made endless lists, names, dates, places – but left out all the colour, the emotion, the real lives behind the faces and addresses. Still, those lists are helping me figure out the relationships, order of birth and all the pieces that go missing in family trees where there are only women to pass on the stories. On the most difficult to reach branch of the tree sits the lesbian.

Of all the sacred places, which has had the most effect on me? It's usually associated with rocks. The rocks in the Flinders Ranges, the scented rock in the Temple of the Rock in East Jerusalem, the rock in the Church of the Holy Sepulchre down another road in Jerusalem, the rock at New Grange in Ireland or the standing stones of Lewis, the hypogeum on Malta, Maes Howe on the Orkneys, the rock at Kata Tjuta, the tears of Pele on Hawai'i, the baetyl stones of Sardinia, the rock on the southern shore of Crete near Agia Galini, and an almost identical rock near Mahabalipuram in southern India. So many rocks in so many places. What is it about rocks?

And the body? Is it a kind of rock?

DESI

Did she ever stay home? And what does this fragment about rocks mean? Is it some kind of list? I want to tease apart strand by strand: reality and fiction. How many dimensions are there? Eleven? For my aunt there are endless skeins wound in ordered chaos. One minute she's writing of kalpas, the next she's reciting Blake on sand and forests. She follows a clue, a single photograph of two women standing on the moors on a windy day. They are not dressed for the moors. Eudy wears a pale suit, gloves, a string of pearls and a hat. Her companion is hatted (I love my love with a hat, said Gertrude) and dressed in a dark suit. She is in profile looking directly at Eudy. There's another of her, a sepia portrait. Her hair is cut in a bob. This one is dated, 1931.

I found in my gran's papers dates for the previous generation. Eudy moved to London around 1920. I suspect Maia's stories of the war – the Great War – encouraged her. Once there she did not return home ever again. I ask why? The most satisfying answer is that exile suited women at that time when London was big enough and anonymous enough to live as a lesbian. With so many men killed in the war, two women sharing a home was common.

She lived in an area that was the centre of old Londinium, destroyed in the Great Fire of 1666. Damaged again in the Blitz. The Ambulance Service was where she worked, assisting the injured and collecting the dead. Perhaps that is when she met Ruby.

It's all in the touch of the bone. Letters in words. Structure is what makes it, otherwise we're toothless flowing like a figure in amber. You'd think that a happy outcome, but what are arms without muscle? Poetry is that muscle.

As epic it is passed down through many generations. It flourishes in metrical formulas. Metaphors are tendons, holding bone and muscle together. Owl-eyed Athena does more than describe her eyes, it provides a way for the poet to keep speaking, finding a way to the next poetic line.

As lyric it sings its way into the heart. Desire flings itself about. The names of flowers and blossoms proliferate, butterflies procreate. Deathless love reigns.

Poetry builds line by line. Letters, syllables and words all count. Some languages allow you to read back and forth up and down. I remember reading a book about Sanskrit poetry. You can create compound words, a bit like those long dense German words which you can never quite understand. In Sanskrit you can add another layer because you can break the words in different places so the long word means two completely different things. They call this *shlesha*.

Poetry is the infrastructure of language. In it are grammars of memory, this and that, stories and myths. It's an organic way of remembering all the necessary knowledge for survival.

Mountains and rocks are a substratum, a place to put those memories, to remind us of deities and ancestors, to bring animals at the right time of year, to make the plants efficacious in healing. Poetry makes all this possible.

Mentifacts are artefacts of the mind left behind by those who went before. You find them in the oldest poems and songs recited and chanted to secure the synapses' snapping connections, creating culture that will be passed down through countless generations without change. Metre keeps it firm.

You find mentifacts in stone circles, carved into rock walls, the handprint and the animal footprint leading the way, the motion of the stars followed by word and rock. Constellations rise and set along the ecliptic of the mind.

You find mentifacts in dance and music, the body's form taking so many shapes, dancing emu on one continent, trumpeting elephants on another. Music trembles, the body is a concatenation of limbs and rhythm.

Pelasgian poetry is as old as the hills. Metre feeds into Homer's words, that blind poet who spoke of the transformation of souls and animals inhabiting another dimension, the dimension of peasant poetry. He carries poems like fruits in a basket, a fusion of colour and sound.

DAY 10

Each time I try to think of the pain, my brain goes blank. It's as though the words that usually roll about endlessly in my head have been wrapped up in gauze, secured away in some corner. Do the brain's synapses prioritise pain over language? Why won't the words come? I remember how I puzzled over pain in my philosophy classes. They asked us to write about the difference between pain and horses. I barely understood what I wrote but the dualist teacher thought I had grasped something in that essay. It centred on the impossibility of knowing the pain of others. The untouchability of pain. I can touch, see, smell, hear a horse and others around me can agree on it. But with pain, we can agree only on the behaviour of the sufferer. This is the theory that the torturers go along with. It creates a distance between what they do and what they see and hear in response to their actions. They allow themselves to say, who really knows whether she is in pain? Maybe she is pretending. Even when we tortured ones die, they can say to themselves, it wasn't pain that killed her. I've changed my ideas over the years. It's not the same as a horse, but we agree on knowing all sorts of things we can't individually verify, and pain comes with reactions. What they did to me yesterday was the pain of indignity. They did not prod me with electrical rods, but it hurt me in other ways. I felt pain in my chest, as if my heart was breaking. They knew this. They know a lot about me and I fear their knowledge. I fear too, what they know about you.

DESI

I've been reading about pain. Trying to understand. Why do some children tear the legs off grasshoppers and others cry at the thought? Is there any connection between this and how they behave as adults? Elaine Scarry says that pain destroys language. Is that behind Kate's ideas about inventing language? It's a kind of revenge against the torturers. Her way of winning.

All I can do is to remain silent. I press my nose up against the wall as a way of steadying my emotions. In that position, the camera can see only the back of my head.

Mercedes, Mercedes, let me dwell on you for a time. You have such confidence in your bearing. When you walk, I can see how you are attached to the earth and simultaneously your tread is light. It's the spirit of the Latin dances in you. Only when you turn, do I see the shadows in those eyes. There are places in you I have never reached. Sometimes it was like walking into a light-filled room and then the light failing. There were no shortages of stories, but thinking upon it now, I think that the stories were a cover-up of the horror years in Chile. You told me your family history, the blood baths, the elopements, the desertions and betrayals. No wonder you all held so tightly to one another. In your universe, the strings were packed tight.

In mine, they floated like the tentacles of a Portuguese man o' war.

DESI

I don't know much about South America. I'm going to have to read up on history. Mercedes came to Australia with her family in the 1970s. In among Kate's papers there are a few heavily marked books, history, some fiction and a few poetry titles.

A bilingual edition of the banned *Evohe* by Cristina Peri Rossi: a book about lesbian desire with a Greek title and an author from Uruguay who went into exile. There is poetry by Marjorie Agosin and Alicia Partnoy as well as stories and novels by Luisa Valenzuela. There's a small stack of multiple copies of *Brujas*, a feminist magazine from Buenos Aires. I look up *bruja* on my phone dictionary, Witch. The resisters of former centuries. By the dates on the books it looks as though she read these long before her arrest and with markings in different coloured pens I'm guessing she reread them afterwards. Now it's my turn.

One page has a giant bird drawn on it. Its black wings spread wide. I have never seen a bird like this. It looks like it has snow on its head.

DAY 11

My mind is obsessive. I have spent hours looking at the crack in the concrete. The way it zigzags down the wall and then branches. I've turned it into a picture of a horse's head. Turned sideways there's something clown-like about it. By the time they finish with me I should be surrounded by a gallery of images. How long will they keep me here? What will they do to me? I try not the think of the possibilities – and yet, my only protection is to try and anticipate, try to think of ways for my mind to exceed theirs.

With my mind's eye I draw up the images of artists. Suzanne Bellamy's porcelain works and her textured prints featuring the lives of Virginia and Gertrude. I turn them over and around, examining the spine of one, the snakes coiling around her shoulders. I hold the small porcelain book in my hand. Its title the kind of book I'd like to read which has not yet been written. *Lesbian Linear B*. The decoding of lesbian knowledge, of the symbols and codes we have used throughout our persecuted history. The author's name is Anonymous. It is Unknown. Where, as Jovette Marchessault asks, is the Tomb of the Unknown Lesbian? Who is she? What shall we call her? Shall we call her Multitude? Shall we call her Offensive?

Mnemosyne, mother of so many arts. Without her we could not have the world around us stored in memory. Memory is underrated these days. People think it exists in silicon chips. But memory is far richer.

Her daughters, Euterpe, Terpsichore and Polyhymnia are best friends. They are in constant movement. They mimic birds with their song. They are forever tapping this stick against that skin, blowing hollow tubes, humming and chanting, their bodies are in free flight. They are the eldest of the arts.

The poets inform them that they need some content, so along comes Erato to put words into the songs and her sister, serious-faced Kalliope, who says if you are earnest about poetry you have to be prepared to stay up all night. The musicians cheer their night-owl sisters.

Next come the twins, Melpomene and Thalia. They claim that their theatrical art draws together all the previous ones, adding that we need to cry and laugh. Melpomene is the older sister, but Thalia always has the last word.

What point is there, chimes in Klio, if you can't organise your collective memory? History is what we agree on; it's what we will pass on to the next generation. Finally comes Urania, who opines that all of this is pointless if you don't organise time. The astronomical bodies, she says, are our best bet. They are regular in their movements; they outlive each small life and we can trace our stories through their motions.

DESI

Ekaterina, you really know your mythology, but unlike you I have to look it up. Here are the names of the daughters of Mnemosyne.

Euterpe: music
Terpsichore: dance
Polyhymnia: song
Erato: lyric poetry.
Kalliope: epic poetry
Melpomene: tragedy
Thalia: comedy
Klio: history
Urania: astronomy
The Tenth Muse is Psappha

DAY 11

So, what did they want to achieve? They showed me their power. Penile power. But also their group bonding as men. Gang rapists. They did not need to touch me to fill me with horror. They are trying to undermine me. I know the self they are trying to inflict with psychic pain. It's my lesbian self. They threaten me with their manhood. They know that I have lived without men in my life for so many years. Someone higher up has read my work. I haven't exactly kept quiet. But none of us really imagined it would come to this.

DESI

I'm going to Buenos Aires and Santiago. They gave me a travel scholarship so I can find out more for my novel and exegesis. So excited. OMG I need to learn some Spanish. My schoolgirl Italian might help, but it won't be enough.

I wish I had paid more attention to my diagonal relatives. It's too late. Kate is gone and I don't know where Mercedes is or even if she is still here. They are strange; they leave large footprints in some places and then nothing, a great big silence.

DAY 12

I can't figure out what time of day it is. They bang away with the CDs so I can't hear the birds. They took away the hood and replaced it with continuous artificial light. I close my eyes and nothing happens. The few snatches of sleep I have are broken by a sudden blast of sound over the loudspeaker. I am trying to keep my mind active and my body too. I've been doing push-ups. I've been trying to imagine I have a show to do. I see myself climbing the tissue, wrapping, moving to the music and the rhythm of the text. I'm trying to do twenty push-ups as many times a day as I can bear. As well as warm-ups and stretches. But my exhaustion pushes me into apathy and sometimes I just sit. Blank.

Nothingness. A flat grey horizon. The grey of smoke-filled dawns with the odour of burning flesh in the air. It's been our flesh as much as anyone else's. Not just once. Think of the virgin martyrs in Rome. Think of the witch era. The burning pyres. Think of the young widows burned in suttee. Think of the Jews and the Gypsies, the asocials like prostitutes, lesbians and those with disabilities, all defiled for who they were not for what they'd done.

In this underworld, I am finding my way through the five rivers of my ancestors. They were not easy rivers to navigate but since those crossing them were dead, it could not get much worse. Except that paradise might not be reachable. And I ask, whose paradise is it?

Before I enter the underworld I have to talk to Charon, that old ferryman. But an equal opportunity program has been in place and it's a ferrywoman this time. She's taken the old name. Has to. It comes with the job. She ferries me across the Acheron. I weep and weep, and weep some more. A lake of tears. The woes of all who have died before me. Mercedes are you there? Does your underworld speak in Greek?

The Acheron is not enough. By the time Charon drops me on the bank between the Acheron and the Cocytus, I am wailing and lamenting everything I've done wrong. I am still calling out for Mercedes and for our beautiful Priya who was shot on the day I was arrested.

Who would have known I had so many tears in me. Tears like blood, bursting out of me.

We have gone round in a circle and returned to the Acheron which, in turn, meets its tributaries Phlegethon and Periphlegethon. The air is filled with a miasma of smoke. My eyes run, not with tears of sorrow, but as if tear gas canisters had been hurled at me. The way is slow as we circumnavigate these two endless rivers. I sleep for an unknown time.

The Styx is commanded by the goddess of the same name. She is a feisty one, so much so that an oath made to her is unbreakable, even if you are immortal or a deity. I make dozens of oaths of revenge. If Styx is on my side I'll be like that misogynist, Achilles, invulnerable. That's if you believe it. For now, I will.

We are soon swooning along a swollen Lethe. I dunk my bottle into its waters. Drunk on oblivion, I forget my losses, my tears and lamentations, my oaths of revenge. Later, much later I will drink with Mnemosyne.

DESI

Kate keeps writing about numbers with her alter-ego Ekaterina this time. The latest is five rivers. I found this to go with that: the five pillars of torture. That's what happens when you trawl through unhappy research on torture. This one comes from a book called simply, *The Manual*.

> **Wall standing:** Forcing the prisoners to remain for many hours in a stress position – spread-eagled face against the wall, fingers high above the head also on the wall, legs spread apart and feet back so prisoner has to stand on toes with weight of body mainly on the fingers
>
> **Hooding:** black or navy coloured bag over head – keep it there – except during interrogation
>
> **Noise:** continuous loud or hissing noises
>
> **Sleep deprivation:** making it impossible for prisoner to sleep
>
> **Food and drink:** depriving prisoner of food and intensifying thirst

This manual was produced by the CIA or the School of Americas or maybe Operation Condor. I can't quite figure it out because my research skills are in literature not espionage!

DAY 13

Torturers are thieves. They steal from us. They demolish us, our creativity. This is the beginning of a path I must try to endure. How can I protect my beingness? How long will it go on? How will it end? I am scared.

Who will I betray? Who betrayed us?

All my dead are beside me: the humans and the dogs. How to contain this grief? They shot my two best friends. Mercedes and Priya. They treated Priya like a piece of rubbish, holding up her body, her muscles twitching briefly in a memory of life, then kicking her. Priya made us smile, waking me in the morning with her wet nose. Waiting for my eyes to open, for me to get my morning act together and make her breakfast. Her body clock was set to our daily routines. Late afternoon, time to remind us of the daily walk, time to visit dog friends. I curl up in this dark and smelly place and try to see her dark eyes, her dingo head, the lovely whorls of hair that meet and swirl like a spiral galaxy.

I think of my ancestors so long ago and how they might think about this journey to an underworld. Like Persephone who cried out when abducted. Only Hekate heard her cries. It's Hekate they named me after. Hekaterina, Ekaterina, Katerina, Kate. What would Hekate do? Ancient feminist that she is, she reports that bigwig Zeus is behind it as is his mafia brother Hades. So what's changed? These old gods are just like their descendant religions. Boys clubs that protect their own.

Hades promises his world to Persephone, says she can be Queen of the Realm. Expects her to be grateful. She misses her mother and wants to visit Demeter. Next is betrayal: *Here my dear, a little red wine with some pomegranate.* Bingo, she is stuck. You're not going anywhere kiddo.

Persephone's trip to the underworld took all the shortcuts. No ferryman to talk to. No one to ask why the hyacinth trapped her on that day. There are plenty of tears. She wails. She beats her fists as Hades carries her over the threshold. It's an unequal fight. She's just a girl. What sort of paradise did he promise her?

There are so many rivers in this underworld. The Acheron, Cocytus, Phlegethon and Periphlegethon, Styx and Lethe meet in a miasmic marsh. A thick fog obscures the way. Each river has its own sorrows. Around me they howl, they cry endlessly, none seems able to stop. My mind is full of forgetting and remembering, remembering and forgetting. I'm not sure which is preferable. Who wants to recall pain? But memory itself hurts when you know she is gone.

Persephone, the stolen child. But not everyone caved in. Kyane was Persephone's best friend. And she was no nymphette. She stood up to the death god who was abducting her friend. Kyane called out to him, *Stop, this is no way to gain a wife let her go.* Hades in self-rapture ruptured earth.

Kyane stood in silence and wept. She wept yet more and with each new tear her body dissolved into fluid. Her hair blue as the sea, melted. Limb by limb, shoulder by arm, she wasted away in grief for her friend.

When Demeter arrived all speech had been swallowed into liquid, no words just bubbling and burbling. She showed Demeter Persephone's sash and Demeter knew the truth of her daughter's abduction.

DESI

I found some more poems by Kate today, they were in a small crumpled envelope. Tucked away. Why? Who was it she didn't want reading these poems? I'm trying to find an order for them – they are tiny poems about love and death and pain.

> Poems are shields–
> they beat my body,
> they prod my skin,
> but my poems are armour, *amor*

I'm not sure what to do with all this writing. It's simply impossible to put it together so that it makes one whole work. Maybe there is some hidden intention. Leaving fragments, leaving her work unjoined. Is it part of her call to the tradition? In fact, even the leaving behind of boxes might be too. What is not acceptable in one era is exciting in another. She wrote some short reflective pieces about her grandmother's generation. Some are auto-biographical, others read like fiction. But who knows? From the family tree, most of that generation died while she was still a child.

Here's another of those tiny poems:

> how to contain
>
> these feelings–
> only poems

Which came first? On the one hand, poetry keeps her sane and protects her, on the other it is the containment of feeling. On the envelope, she had written, *for Mercedes if she ever asks to read.*

My question now, is Mercedes still alive?

Rapunzel and Persephone go out for coffee after the consciousness raising group. Rapunzel says, "I heard your story on the news: abduction, rape and imprisonment. But until we met I didn't connect it to mine. Everyone told me that my mother was a wicked witch. I hadn't realised the lie that contained. They abuse women who try to protect their daughters. She went too far, but in the end she was not so different from Demeter."

Persephone sits nodding, "I didn't know I was being abducted. Uncle Hades was such a charmer. He gave me presents, said we could travel the world. Little did I know that he meant the underworld. His dark hovel. I was relieved when my mother arrived, but even then against her orders I had another red wine and some pomegranate seeds. She was shaking her head saying, "No, don't.""

"And your prince?" asks Persephone.

Rapunzel pauses a moment looks her in the eye, "After your story I'm not falling for that. He too has offered gifts, travel and a kingdom. I'm going to build a tower of my own, keep watch and take myself off on my own travels. Want to join me?"

DAY 14

Two came in for morning tea. They came with a truncheon each. I cowered as they laid into me. I fled to the wall for shelter, for protection. It protected only that part of me pressed against it in fear. They pulled me into the centre of the room. They beat me and beat me. Again and again. They pulled me to them. Pushed me across the room. I hit the wall. When he dragged me up again, he leaned into me, groin first. And smiled as he threw me away like a piece of garbage.

All the stretches and push-ups in the world don't save you from the pain of a truncheon.

DESI

I have found a reference to Mercedes in an old book on women and film. I looked for her films online. They're pretty dark. All about a fictional South American country in which awful things are done to people. My history is not very good. I grew up in the period when history and grammar were ditched from the curriculum. Unless you learnt Italian or French you didn't do grammar. Still, it's clear that what those thugs were doing should have been illegal. But even when it is, they go and redefine legal and illegal so that anything goes. We saw that when George Bush and John Howard were having their cosy little friendship.

It's weird how some dates attract disasters. For my generation, September 11 is unforgettable in how it shifted the world's axis. America needed an enemy, now it had one. But for the people of Chile the same date in 1973 was just as bad. A progressive President, Salvador Allende was assassinated and thousands of his supporters rounded up. Some were taken to the stadium and simply shot. In that same stadium they broke the hands and fingers of singer Victor Jara so he could not play his guitar. But he sang on until they shot him. This was a warning of what was to come under the new regime. Many more would be arrested, tortured until they died or gave up names of contacts. Some survived, most didn't. They acted just like the junta in Argentina, some were thrown from planes, never to be found. The *detenidos-desaparecidos* or the detained-disappeared.

DAY 18

I wake to a silent terror. The cell is cold. The world is verging between black and grey. Featureless. Like fog over an industrial wasteland. Lifeless. Worse. Life destroyed.

The pace is picking up. The night comes with cold and at daybreak the morning violence is repeated. Some days it's beatings. They make threats to my safety. As if I had any from the moment they arrested me.

Hecuba becomes a dog. While most would read this as a demotion, in the form of a dog she was able to escape from the war-riven city of Troy.

Hecuba's life is one of loss, but she was probably a seer. Her son, Hector, was too much filled with his own importance to follow her instructions about not fighting Achilles. She knew he would lose and die.

She was also mother of Cassandra whose ears were licked by the serpent. Cassandra's words were not believed. What is worse? Not to be believed though true? Not to be obeyed though right? Like mother, like daughter.

Dante says of Hecuba that she began barking like a dog. Listen to the howl of the grief-stricken woman. In her howl is much to be learnt.

DAY 21

They like the early mornings. Pre-dawn is their hour. Before bird song. It was the same the day of my arrest. I woke to pounding and then a crash as they forced their way in. They were in the bedroom and hauling me from my bed. All I could see were the dark hoods and covered mouths. They paused for a moment near the bookshelves and pulled books from the shelf. Nothing random. There was Daly, Dworkin, Wittig … I tried to wrench myself free, thinking, it must be some mistake. They can't be serious. But they were and something was pressed against my cheek. I thought it was a gun and I could feel my insides churn and turn. How long is death? How short is it with a gun against your head?

DESI

Looks like someone did a grand tour just before World War II. That must be Ally. I remember hearing that she escaped from Switzerland in a hurry and got to America just before the first sinking of the war by the Germans. Kate's written San Francisco, Paris, London, 38. She must mean 1939. Why didn't she go back to Greece?

Mercedes, do you remember when we were travelling in India and we started talking about physics and multiverses and how the Hindus worked it all out millennia ago. I've had so much time in here to think that I have revisited all the places we went to, all the silences of deserts, the hootings and rabblings of cities, the calls of animals during long nights and short ones. But that day stands out as luminescent in some way. We were sitting by a river, the sun was setting and an old fashioned Portuguese barque was going up river. My mind was on big things because my father had died the day before and that day was his birthday.

"How many universes do you think there are?" I said.

"Five," you answered.

"I've heard there are eleven."

"Do you always go on what you hear?"

"No, but …"

"Look around," you said, "how can there be so many more?"

"It's not just the physicists," I said, getting defensive. "Hindu philosophy says much the same thing. That there are parallel worlds, that sometimes they slide into one another, intersect like matrices. It's about imagination. How could we even think it if it weren't at least possible?"

"But simplicity would suggest otherwise."

"In fact, the Indians went even further. They reckon there are an infinite number of universes. I guess that goes with the idea that the gods just keep on multiplying. Every god has its own little universe. Every individual her own god."

I had been reading Indian philosophy and was filled with my own knowledge and excitement, mixed with grief. But now, I think maybe there was something to it. For each day that passes here, I hope there's another universe in which pain is not omnipresent. I hope there's a universe in which Mercedes is safe. And I ask, how did I get into this one?

Mercedes you are my M-theory, my theory of everything.

I can see the Indian river flowing by, the water a continuous glide, the light on its surface bristling with energy. All I want is to submerge myself in that matrix, to swim, my arms breaking the surface but continuing to float on that iridescent surface of light.

DAY 21

There are days when Mnemosyne haunts me. I wish she would stop hovering around me. I wake from night terrors when they are repeating endlessly all the horrors of my incarceration so far. The skin scars will heal but what remains in my mind is a great blankness filled with futile eruptions masquerading as thought. I am splintering. I am simply meat, bone, hair, skin which they cut and pull. There can be no tenderness. Simply pain and a great white silence.

When I was twenty, death rounded on me. Suddenly, like bumping into a stranger at a corner. I didn't know who she was, and I was overcome. Three days she held me in her arms. I was not scared only confused. I remember almost nothing. It's been a long time between visits but some months ago she came again. Creeping quietly behind me, she said, "Come let's get to know one another a little better." So I went. You can say no to death, but this was an invitation I couldn't refuse. So we sat, drank coffee, then whiskey. We said goodbye at the door of the cafe like old friends.

DAY 21

They used the gun that day. I heard it. Who were they shooting?

It's our underworld where we play and romance, where we talk and dance. Our world isn't visible. The rest of them walk straight past. There's a bar I go to occasionally. It's called Tartarus. Its entrance is tiny, tucked away in the cleft of a laneway. When you go in there's always some husky voice singing some delectable song, the kind of song that makes your limbs go loose with desire. The liquor is sweet and strong, perhaps it's some kind of ambrosia, the stuff of gods.

Mercedes and I used to go there and dance. We'd sweat as we glided around the floor. I fell in love with Mercedes because of how she dances. When I'm with her, I just follow as we swirl and rock and our feet kick up the rhythm. She dances like an angel. Not just any angel, an angel with gravitas. And then there's the tango. You haven't lived if you haven't danced the tango. Of course, there's the rumba and the samba, and they're pretty good too, but the tango in the arms of your lover … it's a version of heaven.

"Where did you learn to do that?" I ask.

"I didn't learn," says Mercedes. "I was born dancing. We all had to learn the cueca, but too much white handkerchief fluttering for me. The tango suits me better. Maybe I learnt it as I learned to walk. I've just always known what to do and how to do it. When we were kids, we were always dancing. That was before things went bad."

"What went bad?"

"Everything. Politics. The economy. The farm. And later the fear."

"Where was this?"

"Oh, in another country. Another time." She looked at me and said, "You want to learn to tango?"

"I thought you'd never ask." And I slipped into her arms and was transported away.

Then she got serious.

"Okay. Your hand here and mine here. Don't think too much about your feet, feel the movement of my hips and just follow."

I look down at my feet.

"No looking down. Never look down in the tango. If your eyes are not in this dance, nor are you and you'll never learn it."

And so the night went, we danced ourselves into one another's lives.

DAY 23

The gun reappeared today. Until now they've concentrated on humiliation and beatings and drawn out pain. I've not encountered this one before. His voice was different. Cultivated. Velvety. Carefully toned. The result of elocution lessons? He walked around me. Slowly. If you want to show authority, the director had said, take long slow paces. I'd had to play an Argentinian policeman in my first show. It was difficult. I felt uncomfortable given the history. But as we were drawn into the performance, as expectations of the audience drew us yet further, I began to enjoy it. That first night with the rain pouring down on the open shed, I finally got into the role. Hammed it up, strutting around, leading with the groin. Laughed about it. And here he is, walking with long slow paces just as any actor would. Complicity. Me or him? Where is the line between him and me? When does acting tip over into responsibility? His voice is caressing me. And I don't want it. Go away. Go away. A refrain stuck on repeat. But he doesn't. He won't. Suppress the sound of his voice. Try to think of nothing. He's stopped. He leans over me. Whispers. Says, *I know what you want.* My mind is retreating. Rabbit fear. His fist punches into my side and I gasp and cry in dry shock. As I plunge into uncontrollable sobbing, he's trying to win me back. He doesn't want anything from me. I know that, but terrified bits of grey matter are grasping for threads. Hopeless hope.

I hear the snap of a clasp. I'm thinking at a million miles an hour. Synapses crashing into one another as they try to cast aside the thought that it was the sound of a trigger. A man playing with a trigger. They do it all the time in movies. We all know the sound. I don't want to die. But I know the sound of a trigger. Clint Eastwood. Heroism. Law and order. Manhood. High noon. The cowboy riff. Emotional aridity. And then there's the other story. The untold story. The Native American side. The woman raped. Law and order. Manhood.

DESI

Why didn't I think of it earlier? I was watching one of Mercedes'
movies online and out of the corner of my eye I thought I saw
a familiar face. I stopped, went back frame-by-frame on zoom
and there she was. Kate was in the film. Of course, that's what
they all do. Friends, relatives, lovers. Especially when they have a
background in performance. I guess it's not too far from narrative
circus to film.

DESI

Anna drove me to the airport and told me to be careful. She gave me the biggest hug ever. I'm on the plane to Buenos Aires. My first stop (after a short airport stop in Santiago). Not sure why I'm going to Argentina first because Mercedes' family is from Chile. I want to go to the city where they dance the tango. I have some contacts there through my supervisor. I hope they forgive me my poor Spanish. They have promised me a night out listening to songs of tango.

I watched as we crossed the pencil shaped Chile. Then rising up below are the Andes, sharp and white. Great walls of ice and rock. In places it looks like a giant pavlova with kiwi fruit on top.

I decide to do a bit of culture before I start looking at the horror places. In my first museum, a small Remedios Varo painting. Really a retablo. Behind the doors, a tower with wings. Lights are on inside and three mother-of-pearl sickle moons above the keep in a downward pointing triangle. Like an advent calendar but with only one set of doors. There are none of the birds Remedios is so fond of in the turret this time, instead the light-filled tower has grown giant gold-leaf wings and taken flight.

DAY 28

He's walking again. Long slow paces. He plays with me. Offers to remove the hood. Says I'll be able to breathe more easily. I want this, but I don't want him any closer. I don't want to agree to anything. He pauses by my head. Breathes. Takes a step. Pauses. Breathes. Takes a step. And another until the slow pacing takes up its own percussive rhythm. He stops and someone else moves quickly across the room towards me. The string that closes the hood is loosened. I can feel the cool air rush in. Light with it. Artificial light. I relax. I drop my guard. Then I'm choking as something is forced into my mouth. Hard. Metal. I choke and vomit releases from my throat. I'm fighting and thrashing. It stops. I'm struggling to breathe through the vomit. They roll me sideways. Can't have you dying yet when the fun's just beginning, comes Velvet Voice. He turns and walks slowly away. The door closes and I'm trying to feel if there's anyone left in the room. It's quiet. Too quiet. I can't move my hands so I shake my head. Feel the vomit on my cheeks. Feel my revulsion against the gun in my mouth. And his thrill at my fear. His relishing of power. The symbolic power of a hard gun.

DESI

Escuela de Mecanica de la Armada is better known as ESMA. The name distracts you, because when you see a word like *escuela*, school, you think of learning; *mecanica* makes me think of the old Mechanics' Institutes that so many Australian towns had half a century ago. *Armada*, makes me think of Sir Francis Drake and a fleet of ships going in to battle. The battles waged at ESMA were of a very different kind.

This Escuela is all about torture. It is about breaking women and men, so they cannot function. Some were forced to betray themselves and others in the most humiliating ways. The guards would invite the women prisoners to go dancing, only to lock them up and torture them the next day. One woman's husband was killed and she was taken out and expected to celebrate and be cheerful. This is an emotional rollercoaster. And if someone later said they had seen you in the company of well-dressed men the night your husband died, what kind of twisted reality would you be living in?

So much pain. There is a low beam here. You need to duck your head to avoid hitting it. But guards would take the hooded prisoners that way; intentionally making each hit her head on the beam. It's about breaking the spirit. There are stories about the pregnant women who were killed twice. I'm having trouble understanding this. The women would be arrested and tortured but not so much that they would die. Not yet. When they gave birth the child was removed and the woman killed a second time, sometimes from all the preceding horrors, sometimes by being drugged and removed from ESMA, flown in planes and after the drug had worn off pushed from the open doors into the sea. Translocation, they called it.

Hardly anyone escaped. Some went into exile. Exile is escape, but it comes with guilt, as does internal exile. So many have died from broken hearts and bodies, their veins cut open. So few remain to speak at the trials that would follow. And when they did there were no women judges, so the women who'd been tortured had to tell their stories to men. Did they tell all of it?

My world is unravelling. It's no longer the flight of a fledgling, I am in freefall. Each time I think, each time I try to think, I hit a wall. Blank wall. Blankness surrounds me. A whiteout. Boundaries have been moved. The boundaries between my flesh and theirs. They have violated those boundaries. They have violated me. And through me, as they know, they are symbolically violating every other lesbian on this planet. Will anyone speak up? I go on. I must.

The cartoon, *My mother made me a lesbian*. The response, *If I gave her the wool would she make me one too*, as mother sits knitting. The making here is in reverse. Here they unmake us. They begin to pull the skein of wool, and as they pull, we unravel. The knitted lesbian is as fragile as the single unravelled stitch. Purl or plain. Ribbed or cabled. Moss stitch or rice stitch. Fair isle or basket stitch. A culture knitted by women. Genealogies encoded in patterns. Our worlds pulling apart. Unstitched.

I have been pulling threads off the edges of my garments. Maybe if I braid the fibres and splice them, eventually I'll make some small rope. And if not, at least it is something to do. It keeps my fingers busy. It keeps my brain from looping too many times in destructive cycles.

If I keep on spinning these threads, like the Norns, will it bring you back Mercedes? Who will weave the threads together so that our lives can continue? Which ancient or contemporary goddess can help? Can anyone help? Remedios understood this with her women in towers weaving destinies, conjuring birds or flying through the air on marvellous contraptions.

DESI

Each morning I go across the street for breakfast. At the cafe they already know what I want on the second morning. "Espresso y medialunas," I chirp in my newest sentence. These *medialunas* – half moons – are small sweet croissants. They also bring an orange juice even if you haven't asked for it.

I sit reading my books for hours and no one moves me on. The reading is intense and horrifying. At ESMA I look at all the faces on the windows. The light shining through them, their names remembered. The disappeared. Impossible to comprehend.

I'm on a boat, sails unfurled. The wind blowing in just the right direction. It's quiet. Not silent, but the quiet of sails in the wind and sea lapping against the boat. I'm heading away from the island into the unknown. All I want is the kind of peace that only nature brings. I lash everything into place, keeping busy. Then I lie back on the vinyl-covered seat and look up at the sky. Tufty white clouds against the blue dome. I sail out and away from the shore, a solitary fool on a ship. The Fool. The one who wants to do things differently. She is dressed in minstrel clothes, carries only a small musical instrument and a sheaf of poems to which she will add from time to time. Her name is Beatrice and in some worlds she lives forever. In this world that won't be so, but she will live long enough to write a new collection of poems. The spinnaker won't swing round and knock her out. She won't drown at sea in a storm. She won't starve or die of loneliness. In this world she sails out from the shore, away from the island. She allows fate to take her. In a few days, settled by the quiet and in luck with the weather she turns round and heads shorewards. The sea is rolling the boat toward the shore. I think it's safe to return. Safe for my mind. I head for the jetty. I throw the rope over the bollards and pull in. I unload the ice-box, the esky and the small roll of books and dry clothes. I turn on the mobile and ring home. She'll drive here while I moor the boat and row myself back in the dinghy. Priya comes flying toward me when she's sees it's me on the jetty. Licks my face and hands and sits and looks into my eyes like there's no tomorrow.

DAY 32

There are too many lines crossed. Lines of self. Lines of the other. They rip through the lines.

I lie on the bed in the cell. Bed is never the right word here. There is no comfort. It is unrelentingly hard. Time rolls on and sometimes I have no sense of it. I get confused. My brain is madly looking for answers to what used to be simple questions. Where am I? What day is it? What time of day? Then come the harder ones. Who are they? Who do they work for? Who brought me here? Where is here? And the cycle begins again. Sometimes I stumble over, Who am I? But that remains with me. When my brain goes foggy on me I try to take myself somewhere else. Into memory. Into the places I have loved. Into imaginary places where no one will hurt me.

He said he was God. He breathed on me and said, "Feel that. It's the breath of God. Truth. Aletheia. Satyam."

DESI

This page fell out and I can't figure out where it goes. Was it Velvet Voice she was writing about?

DESI

Today I walked with the Mothers in the Plaza de Mayo. Reminders of them are there all the time. On the pavement are images of the white headscarves that represent the grandmothers and the mothers. Every Thursday at 3.30 p.m., the Mothers walk around. Some remain seated, others walk. It doesn't seem to matter that they are old. They turn up every week.

All those children stolen and farmed out to the military or their relatives. It sounds clichéd to say I didn't know about this. It makes me think of home and the Stolen Generations.

I grew up knowing about the Stolen Generations in Australia. My parents were okay on this, not brilliant, but okay. They marched on Sorry Day a couple of times. But until now, I hadn't thought of stealing children as an act of war. You hear things about other countries, places like Armenia where children were taken as they fled from the Turkish army with their families. These children grew up Turkish instead of Armenian. But until coming to Buenos Aires I hadn't connected this to aspects of my own life. We always think bad things can't happen in our country. But they do. Thousands of babies removed from young mothers in the 1960s and 70s. They called it social adoption, but really it was theft. Think of all those Aboriginal kids taken from their homes over decades, their families lost in racist bureaucracies. And the others, the refugees, in detention, like a concentration camp. Even the jurisdictions are altered. Island territories excised from Australia. A kind of legal clitoridectomy. What's next, amputation? And then there is Kate's incarceration.

My friends made good on the tango singing. I'd have thought that at 80 you'd be too old to sing the tango. Not Susana Rinaldi. She belted out a string of songs, some lyrical, others like a Spanish version of the blues. In between songs she talked. I wish I'd understood more, but when she sang you didn't need a translator. All the emotion there, right up front. What a treat.

It was a time of disaster. A time of war. None of us was safe. Least of all those who had a history of political activism. Each of us reacted differently. I'm the sneaky kind, good at keeping my mouth shut – except in print. That was my downfall. Mercedes on the other hand speaks out. Everyone knows what she thinks within five minutes of meeting her. She's not brash, just forthright. And determined.

I only wish she would speak to me now. But in her silence she is determined too.

When we met, every day was a summer day. We relished the heat, the sweat, the soft humidity on our skins. But that was before things changed. That was before the nightmares turned into harsh reality. Any dream, no matter how bad, is better than what I have endured.

We travelled to Crete. All the aunts and uncles had left for other places. No grandmothers or great aunts. All dead and buried. So we visited as tourists. Now and then an image from my childhood would lunge at me, but I had never known enough to put everything in place.

Mercedes and I went to Knossos. It was hot. Clear blue sky, almost like Australia. The dry air crept into my nostrils as I walked around this ancient place now tarted up for tourists. An ochre wall, a throne, a series of dolphins like flying ducks on the wall and a truly great view. The air-conditioning came through the windows and breezeways. This was a palace, but it was a palace built with its environment. It was majestic but not disengaged from the surroundings. I loved the place. I wanted all over again to be an archaeologist, to unearth peoples' histories, to make stories about their lives, their passions, their art and architecture. But life takes its own turns and sometimes you finish up facing in completely different directions than those you'd anticipated.

The next day we visited the museum in Irakleion. I walked between the display cabinets, I stood and stared and then you called me over and said, "Look at this." And at that moment the magic of the seal stones opened up. There were hundreds of them, each carved with the same care for detail as an Indian miniature. And the liveliness, the sheer force of those fluid lines. It could have been made yesterday. It felt contemporary, not ancient.

The day vanished as I contemplated one strand of my ancestry and wondered where I fitted in with all of this. Could I come back here? Could I visit Elena on the Lassithi Plateau? Could I live among these people who feel so foreign and yet so familiar?

DESI

Buenos Aires is an odd place. On the one hand there's the tango and a sense that you should join the party when here. But behind this glossy and glassy exterior is something hard. You can still feel the terror in the street. It's not in your face as it is in some places, but can hit you unexpectedly. I've been walking and walking. It's flat, an old river plain. La Boca at the mouth. And then there's the organised walking, so many protests. A huge march about ending violence against women, but as elsewhere it continues. I even saw a sign that said 'LESBIANAS PRESENTES!'.

I'm trying to get my head around what happened in the 1970s and 80s before I go to Santiago and face the places where Mercedes' friends and family suffered. It's not the same, the two countries – Argentina and Chile – but the same forces were at work and I need to understand more so I know what to look for in the real world now.

ESMA really rattled me. It looks so ordinary, banal, as Hannah Arendt would say.

I've come to see that the torturer prefers academic theories to common-sense knowledge. Torture is a distortion. The torturer is not after truth. Not even after information. The torturer wants to break the person who is subjected to pain, uncertainty, disorientation, and humiliation. When it comes to women, the torturer wants to inflict shame on her. To do this he will reduce her to her sex, by which he means her genitals. When they torture a man, the most effective method of shame is to reduce him to the female sex.

Over dinner in Buenos Aires we talked of torture. We talked of what had happened to the lesbians in Nazi Germany. The asocials. We talked of what was happening right now in countries without our freedoms. Maria says that in Colombia, we are called the 'disposables'. And I quoted back to her Gill Hanscombe's poem, 'Sybil's Saturation', which begins, *No one is proud of dykes.* And towards the end, *Only other dykes are proud of dykes.* I fear for our vulnerability, the potential for erasure and disappearance. I am still finding it hard to believe that it can happen to us, or rather that it happened to my Aunt Kate.

Someone at the table said that the profession of accountancy began with the Spanish Inquisition. That the church wanted to count the assets of those they tortured. From inquisition to globalisation. Are we living in some kind of accountant's fantasy world where everything adds up, and those who don't, finish up here? How did Kate add up? Radical, vocal, influential, activist always fighting for the underdog, lesbian, outlaw, ratbag without friends in high places.

Torture is like rape. Rape is torture. If you don't resist, where is their stature as a torturer? If you do, they will drag it out of you, think that they own you.

Yesterday, I went to the Memory Park, a place filled with art that recognises past terrors, including a wall filled with countless names. And as I was walking home, there were tango dancers in the street. Dancing at the intersection of two pedestrian streets. They looked great.

Yet more tango dancers today at La Boca. A tourist rip-off but also filled with colour, even the footpath, lots of brightly coloured corrugated walls. I felt at home with the architecture. I enjoyed the break from all the misery I've been seeing and thinking about.

It is dark, a dark that brings comfort. The air is warm and I feel the breeze off the sea caressing my skin. The air is like a lover. I stretch my head back against the ground, listening to the heartbeat, the earthbeat, the earth-heart. I look directly up into the star-filled night. There they are. The Sisters. I count them. All seven are visible. They are the sisters who bring us the arts. Dance and music and poetry and more. They turn, and rise, pirouette and sink below the horizon.

In the latest tales about them, they have gone feral. They have scored a hotted-up car. An old Subaru with a bigger engine. Instead of fleeing from Orion, they have turned on him. They have bows and arrows. They have slingshots. They have the mask of Medusa to protect them. They are surrounded by harpies and hags, by winged horses and unicorns. They are stampeding in revenge. In that hell called Limbo, the sisters have joined forces with the dykes on bikes from Sydney's Mardi Gras. Together they pound and roar across the desert, sending up dusts of many colours. These dancing sisters have been taking lessons from Kali. They know where to tread. They know the soft parts, the vulnerable places.

DESI

The first street name I see on arriving in Santiago is Merced. That bodes well, I think. I decide to jump in and visit the places on my list as soon as I can. I begin with Villa Grimaldi. Probably the most important of the torture centres run by DINA (the Chilean Secret Police under Pinochet). It's a bit of a hike out there, time to think about too many things.

I am pumped with adrenaline and I rush through the beginning and then come to the Rose Garden. It stops me in my tracks.

The Rose Garden is filled with the scent of rose oil. Each rose has the name of a woman who died here or disappeared. I am walking around with my camera to document it all. The first name I see includes Mercedes; the second has the first name Mercedes. There is of course more to this and perhaps I am just noticing because I know this name so well. I also find the place where women prisoners were held and the *parrilla* room. I shudder thinking about it. The *parrilla*, the grill, the metal frame and the means for electrocuting prisoners. Bodies treated as barbecued meat.

Mercedes, Carmen, Lina, Susana, Aurora, Clara, Ana, Maria, Luisa. They could be the nine Muses. These days the Muses have nowhere to hang out. There are no more unexplored caves or underground rivers or volcanic vents. Humans have filled all the spaces and now there is no room in our psyches for the mysterious.

DAY 35

I don't know what they want. They ask me questions and I don't know the answers. They ask me about others. Those they ask about, I don't know. Is this some kind of trick? Are they making me want to answer them? Are they saving the questions I know about until later? So that then I'll want to scream out the answers? They deny me even that satisfaction.

Each day they unstitch a new part of me. There's the relentless beating. The reminders of the gun. My brain stalls each time I think of it. The pointedness of their violence is increasing. Velvet Voice visits randomly. When I hear his footsteps, the fear rises like vomit. Today they had me spreadeagled on the floor. Face down. Urine filling my nostrils. He paced in a decreasing spiral shape. Laughing at the women who give the spiral such importance. I'll show you what a spiral's for he said. And at that he stepped onto my left hand. Get rid of the left hand, he said. I know you like language games. Sinister sister. At that he stepped onto my right hand. Rosie fingered dawn, you slut. He stepped and twisted his foot heavily over my fingers. No more fingersmithing for you. He stepped and twisted. Paced and stepped and twisted again. The bones broken. The fingers flat and useless just as he wanted. He always leaves me in pain. He always leaves and I'm wracked with sobbing. The horror of what he does. My fingers crushed like broken twigs. My hands rotting stumps. In Iran, I remember, they amputate the hands of lesbians.

DESI

Valparaiso. What a town. It's really crazy. Built right into the cliffs with pedestrian terraces where dogs lie about in the sun. They have no collars, which bothered me until my friend told me that they are owned by everyone, collectively. What a great idea. It helps that no cars can come to this part of the town.

After walking the terraces we visited Pablo Neruda's house. His house is like an ornate poem with lots of surprises inside. It has the best view ever. Overlooking the cliffs, the sweep of the port and the streets along the shoreline. I looked up some of his poems. He wrote about love and forgetting and another about burying his dog. I like their simplicity.

He loved having visitors to share his meals (I wonder who cooked) and he began drinking whiskey before lunch. His study is like the funnel of a ship on the top floor. Out there, I think, a long way away, is the Australian coastline.

There is an audio guide to each room and floor of the house. When the coup came, the military trashed his house. He was ill and taken to hospital. A doctor gave him an injection, at which point Neruda insisted he be taken home. He died less than two weeks after Pinochet came to power. Some say it was the injection that killed him.

As you fly from east to west from Afghanistan to Iran, you cross rugged mountains that go on and on. The colour shifts from the reddish soil of the Indian subcontinent through brown and somewhere halfway to yellow. Then it flattens out and green cultivation follows the rivers. The plots of cultivated land here are larger than to the east. Even cities thrive. And then come the salt pans.

I'm on a camel. We have become a single figure in our lolloping movement. I am the pendulum poised over the rocking base. Our desert trek is taking in the ancient monuments of Hatshepsut and the Temple of Amun. The columns rise above us. Jack was here with his beanstalks. These could be ladders to another a world. Each column is carved and painted. The Egyptian goddess, Isis, spreads her wings, reaching out to encompass the whole universe. Other poets have been here before me. Hilda was one of them. She was transformed and saw a new world. She read the hieroglyphics as if she had written them herself. The years ahead spread out like a map. Would she ever travel the Silk Road? Would she ever sail into her own harbour? What she would do was to revision that ancient world, to see the real story of Helen and of Hilda.

DAY 37

My brain is like a map. A grey and white spiral print with complex twists and turnings. It could be the passage of mitochondria through time, the female line. Now and then a thick red line crosses the branches and my mind stops until I can invent a way around this barrier.

My hands are broken. I can't keep myself strong any more. At least not in my arms. So I stand. I defy them by standing. I begin to walk and pace. I begin to step back and forth. In rhythm. There's a dance step I know and so I tread out the pattern of the dance. For any observer looking in this would not resemble a dance, but for me it does. For me the dance is still in me. I step it out. I'm slow, very slow. And hardly full of grace. My hands ache as I turn. I would collapse in the corner if I didn't feel the need to be defiant. I raise my hands to my eyes and look at the poor broken fingers. They are swollen, purple and red. I keep treading out the pattern I have behind my eyes, all the time my brain is filled with the pain and the colour of my fingers. I will dance. I will dance.

My great aunts would say to me, dance. Dance with your heart. Dance as often as you can. All is well with the world when you dance.

There was a dance the old women and the young did together. It was called the trata. It was as old as the hills, perhaps older. It might have been a dance of creation. I remember the line of dancers spiralling inwards and out again, the women holding hands. One year, I was pulled into the dance. I almost fell over my feet, but everyone held me up and I danced with a thrill in my heart. At the end of the dance, which was a long time coming, all the women trilled and sang like birds.

I now know that this was the dance done at Eleusis. The woman who led the dance represented Persephone. People travelled to Eleusis from all over the ancient world. And they kept its secret. The Eleusinian mysteries were performed for two thousand years. We think our lives are special, but they are short and our memories even shorter.

DAY 42

Who was it in the group who told them where we lived? How did they know to come to our high-walled back yard and in through the door that goes directly to the bedroom. Priya heard them before we did. She was lying on the bed and a low growl was trembling in her throat. As they entered she barked and leapt at one of them. That was the first shot. She died trying to protect us.

DESI

Persephone was another stolen child. The stealing of women and children keeps being told in so many old stories and nothing is ever done about it. The girls captured by Boko Haram are rejected if and when they return home because they are now spoiled goods. Girls in so many places are stolen, raped and forced to marry or clean house; the boys are stolen and sent as cannon fodder for unnecessary wars. Some stories make it sound like the children wanted to go, as in the case of the Pied Piper. A dance of sorts, but more like a death march.

In Argentina, the grandmothers are still looking for their grandchildren. The last was found just a few months ago. Of the known 500 or so, they have found about a quarter. Where are the rest?

In the Tierra del Fuego, the missionaries came, just as they did in Australia and too many other places. The exhibition at the Museo de Bellas Artes shows young women in 1923 with their bodies painted, looking directly at the camera. A year later dressed in heavy clothes, their pride is slipping away. Those young women were stolen by the church.

How can we call an end to the theft of children? How do we prevent women from being carted off in ritual rape?

DAY 45

The days drag by. They leave me here in my misery to watch the colour of my hands and fingers change. I try placing them against a hard surface and pressing ever so gently. But my nerves still scream. I sit and think. I compose more poems in my head. I think of creating something called Theagenesis. A series of stories or poems about creativity and women. It's a high falutin' title, but you've got to do something in here to keep your mind out of the sewer.

The horse's head in the wall has transmogrified again and now what I can see is a giant tulip, or perhaps it's a hearing trumpet. I'll be in need of one them when I leave, my eardrums burst from the noise of Eminem stringing his words into my consciousness. They've got a loop that sounds like: "wanna see that little dyke get swiped out".

The noise is getting to me. Now and then I try to hear the rivers in the sound. Like rivers on a typeset page that create patterns. Or like the horse's head in the wall. Everything creates patterns, but when you are battered by it, it turns to chaos.

In the night, I cry. For myself. My tears are for me and me only.

DESI

The problem of collaborators. They are in every regime. What makes a person betray others? It's complex. In Chile there were many, but only one is really well known. Luz Arce. Along with La Flaca and Carola she assisted DINA in identifying people who were involved in left revolutionary movements. Of these three whose names I know, all were caught in relationships with men in the armed forces. Did they get involved as a shield from violence? Or was it more like the dynamic of domestic violence, a cycle that spirals out of control? Women get into relationships with men for protection, but that very relationship becomes their greatest vulnerability. Collaboration for women in these circumstances is full of the power of love, fear, protection of others and self-preservation. Luz says it was because she feared for her son's safety. Does that excuse her? Lesbians are not perfect, but few of us fall for the idea that a man will rescue us and make us safe.

The doors to the underworld are closed. Naked people, like figures from a Bosch painting, wander aimlessly. I undress and head down the stairs. Every door I try is closed to me. Others go in and emerge, climbing the stairs to the surface. A large room with couches opens and I walk towards a circle of soft lounges. The room is big, like an old-fashioned railway waiting room. A large German shepherd approaches and lies down next to me. Two women sit down; they look like mother and daughter. The daughter hugs the dog who rolls over on its back, all vulnerability. I stand and walk towards a door that has opened for me. But the dog bounces across the room and stands in front of the door, blocking my path.

The mother of the underworld is Chaos. She lies in the space between time and space. Chaos is so insubstantial she needed something to hold on to and so she created Earth (Gaia) and the Underworld (Tartarus). Gaia is strong and trustworthy. Tartarus allows almost everything: love in the darkness, love all night.

DESI

The underworld is right here now. It was here after 11 September 1973 too. Londres 38. I was there yesterday. It looks like a respectable street, cobbled stones, a few hotels, coffee shops, a quiet area to relax in. The house itself is not that big though there are several levels. And it is close to the buildings around. But it is raw. Unlike ESMA, this is not sanitised. You can feel the terror in the walls. I went upstairs and looked across the street to the window boxes with flowers. A door that can't be opened. Sounds of beatings and screaming. Could the neighbours hear? Did they not want to hear?

Over dinner, I asked my supervisor's friends about the street. How come no one seemed to know about it for such a long time? And why did no one hear the screaming?

"It was a red light district," came the answer.

What brothel owner is going to say anything? They were probably paying money to the police and DINA. Better to keep your mouth shut than upset the 'customers'.

And then the penny dropped. I remembered the note among Kate's papers. San Francisco, Paris, Londres 38. As soon as I returned to my room, I dragged out first the street map which shows that from the street called San Francisco you turn right into Paris and right or left into Londres. My notes are all wrong. I can see now what I had done. In my ignorance I had corrected it and written, *San Francisco, Paris, London 38. She must mean 1939.* I thought it was about our family history.

She didn't mean 1939, she meant this address, this building: Londres 38. Why? She never came to Chile. But Mercedes and her family fled Chile. Again why?

I want a Thesmophoria. Three days off to ascend the mountain with a pack of women. Our backpacks filled with picnic foods: dips, breads, salads, fruit, sweets accompanied by wine, spirits and water. Only on the third day do we eat meat – and some refuse it.

On the second day we fast, apart from nibbling on pomegranate seeds. Beware those fallen on the ground for they are considered dead. Women sit on picnic rugs howling in one another's arms. Grieving all the losses of the last year. By afternoon we are swearing and insulting one another. All the aggro from the last year stored, stirred up and released, like the rushing underworld rivers carrying flotsam and jetsam. Our emotional wreckage is swept away.

The final day is one of creation. We sing, dance, recite our poems. Some daub their faces with coloured clay. The musicians are run off their feet with requests. Most of us eat meat on this day. Creation and decreation. Beautiful birth, she is called, Kalligeneia. When the sun settles into the valley, we descend carrying burning torches.

DAY 46

Time. In this animal stall it feels flat. The kind of time you imagine confronting in Limbo. No beginning, no end and a multiplicity of middles. I have always thought of time as my friend. But we're no longer on such good terms. Time spins me around, disorients me, tricks me with her insubstantial forms and her combined simplicity and complexity. Endlessly elastic. One moment like a dense ball, another floating free as a will-o-the-wisp. It's the dense ball times that are the hardest to bear. Bound. Depressed. Chained. No escape. An internal pressure that bears inwards more and more. Until I'm nothing. A dot of almost being. All I can do is sit, or sleep, or collapse.

In the midst of a time of almost being, they came and dragged me out. I was more rag doll than human. The room of the broken fingers. My mind fled. It spun me out of my almost being into fear and panic. But what kind of life is this, where only fear can kick-start the day?

What happened next, I cannot recount. No, I don't want to speak it. I don't want to put it into words. What if my words are misused? What if in speaking I harm others? My silence adding to the mounds of silence. But what alternative is there? I cannot speak.

The world is flat. I am flat. Time is flat. To admit to anything else is to risk life. Where can I go? Into some mythical time? In that time, that place, nothing can hurt me. It's a place of refuge. A harbour of safety. The sea is flat, but this flatness is benign. The sea is flat and beneath the surface is life in a multitude of shapes, some of them almost unimaginable. The deeper you go, the weirder they get. With little lamps extending in front of their mouths. I need a fish with a headlamp. Not a bicycle. The sea is flat and I am floating down through it. Near the top, it is luminescent. Colourful fish swim by like a pack of women. Others travel singly or in pairs. Their sides, rainbow-streaked. Parrot fish. I am floating free in this warm tropical water. I am swimming back forth and around, over the bommies. Mushroom and brain coral dot the shallow sea floor. I am suddenly hit by the realisation that I can move in a full 360-degree turn. I roll over, turn, spin. It is a 3D world after all.

And then I am drowning. I am being pushed down. My bicycle thrown on top of me. Holding me under. Using the wheels and handlebars to keep me there. I gulp. I strain. I want my breath. I can feel it in my larynx. In my glottis. At the source of my speech. I am asphyxiated.

DESI

I'm back in my small airbnb room near Bellas Artes working through the material I gathered. Looking through my photos, I begin again at Londres 38. On the wall, some lines in Spanish written by one woman to another.

> I remember when I knew you in the house of terror …
> In those moments in which there was light, a dream.
> Or a miracle, though you were that light in the darkness.
> We were a setback. Today thousands of setbacks.
>
> Later, I see you now as you will be today in some place
> always looking ahead.
> We will find one another through the fog that we will clear.
> Do not forget me.

Letter written for Muriel Dockendorf Navarrete, detained and disappeared by her friend Sandra Machuca on 10 October 1974 while both remained detained in the camp of Cuatro Alamos.

In another room:

> What happened in this house,
> happened outside of it,
> the terrorism of the state
> occurred across the whole country.

I cried my eyes out, then tried my hand at a poem of my own.

she is a bird
floating high
or is she falling?

her body is an apron
her arms are wings
insomnia pulls me skyward

night is full of silence
bodies hurled from planes
into the spinning air

DAY 50

I don't know what happened after that session. I came to back in the stall. As usual it was dark. The battering music was playing. The room was filled with noise ghosts. I could see their long filament bodies floating in the room. Something between a dragonfly and a skeleton. It took a long time for me to feel my body. The fear of feeling. A lump of clay before life was breathed into it. Pre-Titan. I felt it from the inside and it felt bruised. It felt like a potato with its insides mashed. I think I fell asleep again without moving. The brain retreats. I think there were a series of wakings and fallings. Each time the ghosts were there. Each time I felt another small square of my body. Flat. The word 'flat'. Feeling like all the air had been squeezed out of me. And I was flat. Had they run me over with a psychic steamroller? I lifted my hands slowly and placed them on my ribcage. My chest felt narrower, flatter than usual. And each tiny pressure hurt.

The pain reminds me where I am. I am a prisoner and I don't know when this will end. The me is tiny. It is like a grain of sand. That Blakeian universe. It is like birdsong beginning inside the egg. A strand of hope. Is that what Rumi was on about? Can hope grow out of pain? Do I have a future? But the uncertainty. Will it end? Or will this stall be my grave? What is worse? Death? Pain? Uncertainty? The last.

DESI

In the Museo de la Memoria y Derechos Humanos my emotions are flung around. The name is not only about memory but the need to uphold human rights, to remember that for so many their rights were flagrantly violated. It's there again where I see the huge black-winged bird with its snowy head. It's the condor. A vulture. Worst of all, this magnificent bird was stolen by the CIA and others in a program called Operation Condor. That's what they do. They steal all the images of power, distort and mangle them and turn them back on the weak and poor. The countries where the Andean Condor was part of art and religion for thousands of years had it turned on them in an attack led by the CIA.

I feel so exasperated and angry. I want to talk to Kate. I want to know what happened and how did her life connect to what happened here in Chile. Where was Mercedes in 1973?

DAY 51

If my name were Peter or Stefano or Abdul, how would what they do to me be different? Their hatred would be different. They would still hate me, but the woman would not be in me. Take that out and they hate differently. What kind of fear is it? The psychologists say that it is engulfment. I disagree. I think it is power. Their fear of their own power. Or that they won't have it. Then what? How will they get to do what they want to do? Have they never heard of love? Have they never wanted to do something for another for the simple pleasure of seeing a smile, of bringing joy? Who are they? Is it all of them? No, but those who have learned well, achieve too much. Their success is the end of their humanity.

I have to think. I have to get out of here. How? The easiest way would be to do what they want. But what is that? None of their questions make sense. In the midst of pain, between consciousness and coma, who knows what I have said. There are gaps. Gaps between my sensible self and the one caught in insensibility. There's a moment when I am all there, and just beforehand I wasn't. So what is the difference? What makes the synapses remember one instant and not the previous?

DESI

I'm on the plane working through the notes I scribbled down. In my head there is the image of the metal bed on which prisoners were placed. It was in the Museum of Memory and Human Rights – and no photos allowed. I find that pictures in my head are often sharper. This one especially. It looks like a shearer's bed without the mattress. Metal. Narrow. Plenty of places to attach electrical conductors. In Villa Grimaldi there was a women's room of detention. Right next to it the room where the *parrilla* was used. Think of it as the common outdoor barbecue. This domestic appliance is turned against the prisoners who are tortured. How do you ever escape the torture when most households have one; when restaurants have *parrilla* emblazoned on their neon signs?

DAY 52

I am nine and sitting in a tree. The day is hot. The smell of wheat dust is in the air. Only a few days before Christmas. And I am angry. So angry I have run away. I want them to know that I am gone. I want them to worry. I sit and sit. My mouth is dry. I don't have any water. When you run away, you just run. You don't prepare for it with water and cut sandwiches. Why aren't they coming to look for me? Why can't I hear them calling? Maybe they don't care. Maybe they are glad that I have gone. I pick leaves off the tree. Tear them along the veins. Scatter them from the branch, watching them float down like confetti. The bark tears under my fingernails. I see how long a strip I can tear without it breaking. I hang the strips over the branch on which I am sitting. I knock them off the branch one by one. Anyone walking under this tree would have to wonder what caused this mess. But no one comes. It is quiet. The day stretches out lazily, rolls over and sleeps. No one cares.

I wonder what they know? Do they know I'm here? Do they fret? Are they doing anything to get me out? How long can I sit here, do nothing, vegetate, wait? I stare at my hands. They'll never be as they were. I dare not look at the other places. I can feel the bruising. I can remember the searing pain. Shafts of metal. The little finger on my right hand doesn't bend. It sticks out at a peculiar angle. Estranged from the finger next to it. Will you come looking for me this time?

DESI

Have you ever looked at a mediaeval manuscript up close? You should. I've been practically living in the university library. Scouring books I never knew existed. They've had an exhibition of manuscripts. My eyes trace the shapes. Monsters inhabit every letter. Snake-bodied women crawl over the letter S. Hair grows all over their bodies like poor St Agnes. Some eat fruits you've never seen unless you're a connoisseur of durian. Women are winged or have wild hairstyles, wilder than goths and punks. A woman cosies up to a lion and a winged horse lounges in her four-poster bed. Acrobats do handstands and contortions around herbal recipes for flying ointment. This is a surreal world that Hieronymus Bosch must have been familiar with; he just didn't bother with the texts.

There was one evening in Buenos Aires when I found myself in Borges Street. This story I am following is like those old manuscripts with their snakes or that garden of forking paths, or underworlds and infernos. Kate keeps referring to Monique Wittig whose Acheron I could be trying to cross. Perhaps I am meant to get lost as we do in weird labyrinths. Oh hell, it's like going back 5000 years to Crete, to boustrophedons, acrobatic leaping of cows and so much more. The records left by the women who were tortured here are just as complex, lots of false clues, dead ends and great chasms that fall away. You could die, as so many did, and no one would know. It's weird but the story that really knocks me around is the one in which the guards take a group of women out dancing at night. They expect them to eat with gusto the food cooked on the *parrilla*, to dance and smile.

And then they take them back, lock them in and next morning beat them up. This is not just physical warfare, but a way of breaking the women psychologically.

DAY 53

The stories in my head have gone away. I can't remember them. It's as if my mouth has been stuffed with a handkerchief. My story blocked. My whole world suppressed. Is that it? They don't want answers. My answers have no relevance. Because what I have to say is not real.

So why am I here? Because of my effect on others? They know what they need to know of me. It's already out there. I have already written it down. I have spoken it, performed it, spun it out in many different ways.

They do what they do as punishment. And as deterrent. If they already know what I know, maybe I can ignore their questions. Maybe I can begin to give nonsense answers. That's what they think I am anyway. Non-sense. As far away from what they see as sense in their limited little world. The one world. The one way. The one god. The one man. The One.

DESI

Among her papers are scraps of undated writing. At least she arranged most things into boxes with dates, though some seem out of place. It's the scraps that have me intrigued.

Codex psapphistra

What could it mean? A kind of imaginary encyclopedia about lesbians. She contemplates writing in Nüshu. She describes a range of animals from a lesbian-centric point of view. She is creating a universe in which lesbian symbols lie at the centre.

a nonsense idea
non sense
only maniacs would dream such things
a pillow book of nonsense dreams
a papyrus of unwritten words
a shard fallen from space
like a meteoroid bringing life
making passage through
the double disk dark matter zone

dingoes will talk
trees will walk
seas will dry
just as likely

imagine
that's what she said
imagine a different world
not the one outside your door
not the one at the top of your brain
turn everything over
create an imaginary world
with imaginary animals and words
create a time when the impossible
becomes possible

DAY 54

I have to speak. I have to get out and speak. I have to survive so that I can speak when I get out. Who do you speak to in solitary? I will speak to myself. I will speak gibberish if I must. If that's what it takes to save myself.

Let's begin.

I am ambushed by memory. What happened the day they brought me here? I was asleep when they broke in. Mercedes and I were both asleep. They were like nightmare ghosts. All neck, only the eyes showing. They dragged me from our bed and as I turned to look back, I saw one of them raise his gun. He shot. Mercedes flinched and I was pulled from the room. Did she die? She must have. But what if …? I have to survive to get out of here. I have to survive to find out.

I say it out loud. They have killed her. Have they killed her? What have they done to her? Who knows? Who cares? Does anyone?

I am a nonsense I do not exist or if I do I am illegal and should be punished killed if need be in China I live and die in the realm of flies in my own land silence is preferred self-suffocation of words my history is full of horizontal lines none are vertical my position in the family is at the far end of a fragile twig ready to break from the main stem in the desert lands my bones are broken whipped into the centre of a sand storm vanished as if I have never existed under dictatorships I am among the first to be crushed my independence my nonsense a threat to social stability I fly from the trapdoors of planes no parachute to break my fall only the sea to catch me in its hardened arms in the cold lands they call me an artist sell my soul to that grumpy old Mephistopheles who's never satisfied no matter how far I go I remain exotic a work of theatre at the centre of the empire the words are decorated with ribbons of acceptance dissertations are mined to snuffle out meaning there's betrayal in those awards in so many places records are changed the archaeologies rebuilt and reshaped to other realities today I was murdered by someone sent by the government

DESI

A small box of photos, black and white. I'm turning them over slowly since I don't know these people. In the background of one is a house. It makes me pause and then I think I recognise this house. It's in Valparaiso. I search online. Yes it's Neruda's house. I turn it over and in faint pencil I see *casa de Pablo*. She must mean Pablo Neruda. I look at the people in the photo. A woman who looks like Mercedes but it can't be her. Who is it? There's also a small girl in the photo.

DAY 64

You think you're a high flyer? That was what they said. They took me to the broken fingers room. They know now that I fear the room itself. They can see me shaking. I try to hide it, but that just makes it worse. Velvet Voice was there. Look what we've got for you today. Training. He pointed to a bar two metres above the floor. A trapeze of sorts. Okay, he said, ten chin-ups. The guard lifted me and my hands flew up automatically. I tried to forget how to do it, but my fingers – except the little one on my right hand grasped the bar. It must be some orang utan memory. I did as they asked, hoping it would at least make me stronger. But so little strength. One was my limit. Then a half. Come on, he said, you can do better than that. We saw you doing push-ups. That was before you stood on my hands, I wanted to yell. My body was remembering and reacting but my strength had gone with my fear and I dropped to the floor. Shall we help her? The guard moved to the wall and lowered the bar with a pulley. It was now at head height. Up you go, he said. Hang by your knees. I stood there thinking what is this? He pushed me. Two more guards came and lifted me as I kicked. But I was no match for them. My knees were over the bar and their hold on me was vice-like. Monkey roll, said Velvet Voice. One grasped my right arm, forcing it under the bar, pulling it toward my shin. The left hand was brought to meet it. They tied my wrists. It reminded me of the no escape position of the sheep my father used to kill. Tie three legs. Here I was with wrists tied. My shins caught under my arms. My arms caught by the bar. No escape. The bar pushed hard against my forearm. I had to try and stay high. But how long can I hold it in my belly? How long can my wrists hold me? As I'm thinking this, the bar is hauled higher. It jolts me and the pain is unbearable. The bar spikes the backs of my knees. It pulls me downward. Gravity assisting in this torture. My wrists are breaking. My forearms cut through. I can't hold it. I can't bear it. I feel my body slump. I'm wracked with weakness. The tears are running down my forehead. Velvet Voice is receding. He is telling me something about a performance. Your best yet, he says.

DESI

All the men are brutes and all the women are birds. It's true. If you read back through your Greek stories, it's all there. I never knew this stuff until I started going through Kate's papers. My favourite is a woman not bird, but perhaps monster: Echidna. The biologist who named the Australian echidna must have been having a bad day. Or perhaps it was just that he couldn't get close enough. I found a puggle one day, baby echidna, still soft around the gills. Have you tried to pick up an echidna? Puggles are not so hard, but adults. All those prickly spines. And how do you tell how old an echidna is? The Greek Echidna was ageless and deathless. Try kissing an echidna! But someone did because Echidna gave birth to two dogs, Orthus and Cerberus and to multiple-headed Hydra. Faced with all those spines you want to have either a mouth full of sharp teeth or a neck full of heads. Especially if she was your mother. Mixed births seem to have been a family tradition because Hydra then gave birth to Chimaera, a dragon figure composed of lion head, goat body and serpentine tail. Maybe that ancient Echidna laid eggs. And now Dr Bogen wants to turn me into an echidna, laying eggs, producing chimaeras and other biotech wonders without even pausing to ask me if I want to lay all my eggs for him. ECHIDNAS UNITE AND REFUSE TO GIVE UP YOUR EGGS. Or we'll send our relative Styx to deal with you. She's as quiet as a thug with a silk handkerchief. You'll wake up on that other shore and never be able to go home again.

DAY 68

Everything I've ever loved is used against me. I was strung up like an old piece of meat. An Inanna ritual gone wrong. This god, this Velvet Voice, who can do anything, did not want me returning from that underworld horror. I've seen carcases treated more gently. I don't know how long I was there. Heavy metal sound pounded my head after he finished talking about my performance. Time again, becoming enemy. Time turning eternal. An eternity of pain. What point is there once I've passed out? What point is there to all of this? The punishment regime. His eyes sparkled with pleasure when he saw that I had understood what they were doing. Monkey roll, he repeated. One of your favourite moves, I hear. No, never. A momentary position to pass through as quickly as possible. Not a position to hold. Not ever.

The pain is stretched through me. My shoulders caught by the stress. My forearms striped with bruises. My guts wrenched from trying to hold myself up. My wrists, exploding with pain. The backs of my knees, vulnerable and bruised. My head aching. What will they do next? Will they fill me with electricity?

DESI

My eyes are practically popping out. I spent most of the day trawling the National Film and Sound Archive for traces of Mercedes. They were a dark lot, the early filmmakers. Not much into narratives, except for Mercedes whose stories were filled with references to Latin America, to hopes followed by horrors. There's a snippet shot in b&w It shows an alleyway, women dancing the tango, their bodies pressed up close. In the middle of this a single shot rings out. A woman falls, is caught in the arms of her lover. A drawn out pause of stillness as if the universe has come to a standstill. A moment later an explosion of movement as women run in all directions. It's like a representation of the big bang. After the running, a fade to darkness.

The film is dated 1977. Mercedes came here in the previous year. There are posters from around that time showing a group of women on the back of a ute with film equipment. Bulky old cameras and sound recorders. They must have bought them secondhand.

My grandmother, Cassandra, made films too. Not many. Mostly home movies on a 16 mm camera. The camera came down to me through Kate. It's small for its time (1934) and not that heavy.

DAY 69

I want to go home. I want to know what happened to Mercedes. I want the world. I want something more than these pain-filled nights. Something more than the smell of urine in my nostrils. How can they get away with this? Who is saying, Okay, go ahead? Whose authority keeps me here? And where is Mercedes? Is she buried in some place, not to be discovered? What was in the papers in the lead up to this? There was no major announcement, but small incremental instances of hatred. I noticed that people seemed to feel freer day-by-day to express their hatred. That those politicians who pronounced Biblical support for their hatred were cheered. Not only that, they were elected. Only a few of us spoke about these thousand cuts to our integrity. I wrote about it in small magazines. No way would the mainstream see any relevance in what I had to say. The socialists and the liberals, the conservatives and the fundamentalists were all in agreement on one thing. They didn't need our vote. Indeed, they didn't want it. Didn't want to be associated with us in any way at all. The small outcry from Jewish lesbians, from radical feminists, from women working against violence had no effect at all. No one listened. We gathered to discuss the situation. But we were few. We wanted to do something public. To shout our fear to passers by. On that day – how long ago was it – a hundred or so of us turned up. We had banners which screamed: LESBIANS KNOW WHY THEY FEAR US. LESBIANS ARE EVERYWHERE. THERE'S A LESBIAN IN YOUR FAMILY. LESBIAN PRIDE. STOP VIOLENCE AGAINST LESBIANS. LOVE A LESBIAN TODAY. Nothing happened. The police stood still and took photographs of us. Passers-by crossed the street. On the news that night, there was no report. We were surprised and puzzled. Should we do it again? All week we walked as if trying to slide away from an enemy in the dark. Apart from us, no one mentioned the demonstration. We had just begun to sleep properly, and then they came. It was a week before they pounced. That was the night they brought me here. That was the night ... does anyone know I'm missing? Will this silence kill us?

DESI

Dark matter is almost imperceptible. Invisible and yet it takes up space. Like a lesbian in a room full of people. She too takes up space. But who sees her. Visible and yet not. Just like Mrs Gardiner. Scientists say that dark matter is all around us, that the energy of ordinary matter is five times less than that of dark matter. I know lesbians like that who have energy five times greater than that of ordinary people. It's not that they are not there, but no one is paying attention. Social obliviousness.

The other thing is the impact clefts that lesbians produce. They are capable of knocking the earth sideways, of creating perturbations in the matrix of life.

Scientists try to measure the amount of dark matter in the universe. I want to measure the number of lesbians. Both are equally elusive. How do you spot a lesbian? Only a lesbian seems to have the right antennae for it, and if you do that someone for sure will say your measure is biased. No one seems to notice the bias that goes the other way or that heterosexuals are forever measuring heterosexuals and they haven't even noticed they are doing it. Oh the frustrations of being a marginal voice! I think I'll just walk out with my head in the Oort clouds and try not to notice. I'm going to be like Eris, cause strife in the outers.

DAY 70

It was fantastic. A storm. A huge storm with thunder clapping directly overhead. I cheered at the break in monotony. I cheered every clap as it shook these deadly walls. I cheered again when all the lights went out. It feels like a renewal. I could hear running footsteps in the hallway. It seems to have thrown them. The unexpectedness of it. They believe so much in their ability to control everything, but they can't control nature. Mother nature, sister nature, thank you.

Rape. I didn't call it rape at the time. I called it stupidity. But in fact it was rape. Rape in the back of a truck. It stays with me like a shadow behind me, like dark wings beating slowly. I turn and the wings seem to lift, but they never leave. They are silent wings. Dark against darkness. He had a pseudonym. Fotoski. Was he Polish? No one ever called him anything else. I met him when I was twelve. He took the photos for day tickets. His beard pecked with snow. My imagination took over. To live in snow country, to work on the snowfields. It was my adolescent dream. So when I remet him five years later in the pub we frequented, I knew him immediately, remembered the cleverness of his name. But of that night, I remember very little. Perhaps we drank in the same group on several occasions. It was not far to walk home, and he offered to drive me. I got in. And when we came to the square close to my home he invited me into the back of his truck. Taken by some curiosity about this man who had access to winter-long stays at the snowfields, I climbed in the back. It was dark, and so he turned on a torch. I don't recall the lead-up, I remember only the rape. The mattress hard against my spine. The top of the truck looming over me. The torch turned off at some stage. I say, No. No. No. He does not listen, he does not speak. He forces me. Holds my hands hard against the truck. I'm crying when I get out the back of the truck. I walk towards the wall and simply stand there. I do nothing. I watch as his truck drives out onto the street. I lean against the wall. I'm a mess. I straighten my clothes. I rinse my face in the water fountain. I wait in the garden for twenty minutes before going in. No one is there.

I spoke to no one about Fotoski. No one. Not even my best friend. And we shared everything. She'd left early that night. I pushed the memory away. Refused to think of it. Although I do recall looking out my window the following morning, noting the exact spot where the truck had parked. Remembering, and then turning away from it. I ate breakfast and set about forgetting. Years later, I finally told Mercedes.

DAY 71

It was rape on the day when the filament ghosts came. The day they beat me flat. They raped me. Velvet Voice watched. He watched while the others came at me. Each one punched me, bit me, pressed me under his weight. Each one had his singular punishment for me. They repeated words of hate "motherfuckin' bitch", "nun slut". Their hatred pierced me. They were having fun. Hooting and egging one another one. "How long's it been?" "You should be grateful. It's what you need. It'll make you a real woman." "Someone should've cured you a long time ago." They were filled with their righteousness, their own sense of truth. Their right to women is their religion. "It's nature," they say. "That's just how God made us." They are simpletons. Not because they lack brains, but because they've never understood that they are not the centre of the universe. They've never taken responsibility for the consequences of their actions.

That day was filled with pain. And the days that followed the trapeze torture have crushed me. But the thunder has cleansed me. Brought a new freshness to the world.

DAY 78

The interrogation continued today. The lights came back on and they were in before I could use the bucket. It was a different room. A room with a screen. "Who are these women?" they barked. I looked as a series of faces flashed by. I did not try to recognise them. I tried to let them pass me by without any response in my eyes. Until, that is, they flashed up Mercedes face. "Who is she?" I shook my head. "Who is she?" A guard grabbed the back of my neck and squeezed, repeating the question. I remained silent. They know full well who she is. Why are they asking? "She's dead," I said. And all the tears I have suppressed streamed from my eyes.

DAY UNKNOWN

Then they released me, unexpectedly I was out. I was lost. I was broken. Like that little doll my aunt used to tell me about. That poor little doll dear. Thrown upon the rubbish heap, questioning life, questioning love, wondering whether love had any part to play now. Can you tell me, Mercedes? Is love part of it? Or has that gone? Please don't tell me if it has. I'm not sure I could bear that. Not yet. My longing for you kept me going.

DESI

The masks. Masks from so many places. Kate would have loved them. There were cows from India and Italy. From across South America, the most colourful of all. It reminded me of Greek drama, the masked actor. Or kids' parties where you try to hide and be someone else. We wear our masks for fun and for protection, for disguise and for spying. We have worn animal masks for millennia. These cow masks protect me and the spirit of Ekaterina in these pages. May she walk the boustrophedonic path back and forth.

Like the underground meetings of women. The catacumbas of Buenos Aires, the feminists who refused funding to ensure their independence from the state. Women gather underground in one another's houses, cafes, bars, even in plain sight where secrets are passed mouth to mouth.

Who will unmask us?

DAY UNKNOWN

There should be something I can do. I am out now and flailing. The walls gave me structure. Even what they did. I could hate them. Or I could tell myself I was better than them. That I would not sink to their level of depravity.

I don't know why they let me go. Ran out of excuses? They dumped me at the edge of a country town. Big enough for no one to notice me. Small enough to be irrelevant. So it was unannounced. I couldn't think of anyone to ring. With Mercedes dead, where could I turn? I stuck out my thumb and when a woman pulled up I got in and breathed out with relief.

"Heading to the city?"

I mumbled a yes, out of practice with talk. She had plenty to talk to me about so there wasn't much silence. I tried a smile when she dropped me in North Melbourne.

I walked and walked until my legs no longer supported me. I took a tram up the Sydney Road hill, too tired to care if a ticket inspector got on.

I went home to Tinning Street and kept a low profile. Sometime in the last two and a half months someone had cleaned the room, thrown out the broken chairs and table. Everything belonging to Mercedes was gone. There was a great empty space in the middle of the living room. Like the empty space inside me.

For several days, I made sure no one was in the street when I went out, or I went out the back way. Because there had been no media, no one knew. I guess, if anyone noticed we weren't at home, they thought we'd gone away somewhere. Not that unusual.

At the ATM, I checked behind me before sticking in my card. It worked. No one had cleared my account. A couple of payments for some love poems in an anthology, and another in a poetry journal. Otherwise, not much movement.

Outside my window the city, once home is now a place of fear. Shadows leap the wall, break down the door. I believed the myth that we are safe in our beds, that our worst fears will not come to fruition. I cry and howl under the sheets. I cry for the arms of Mercedes. For the body warmth of Priya. Grief for all I was throttles me. I forget who I was, who I might have been. Each time I leave the house, the streets are filled with despair like a great festival of wretchedness and desolation. In the garden, rocks sing mournfully their daily dirges. I used to think the world a joyful place but civilisation has destroyed all joy. I howl and wail for the future.

One night I wake screaming because they are about to kill Mercedes again and yet again. She is screaming. I am screaming. I hear the howl of a dying dog. In the din there is the sound of a gun.

Eventually, I rang José. Odd, you'd think I would ring one of my friends, but I wanted someone with more distance who wouldn't expect anything of me. He came to visit. The key was still in our old hiding place which he knew.

Then he told me. He told me Mercedes is alive.

Querida Mercedes,

I thought you were dead. But they tell me – your mother, your brother – that you are not. That somehow you survived that night. I don't know how, because I saw you fall. I saw you fall and I was sure you were dead. So much so, that when they interrogated me, on that one thing I was convincing. The pain of your loss was excruciating.

It's months now since I got out. I went into a state of oblivion for most of that time. I have lost days, weeks – whole layers of memory are fragmented. I have a continuing sense of horror of what they did to me. I am torn between a longing to forget and finding a way to document it.

But for now, that is not my purpose in writing to you. I am writing because I want so much to speak with you. And all the doors are shut.

Your mother, understandably protective of you, says you don't want to see me. She says that all your troubles were brought on by me. I don't know if it is her speaking, or you. And I need to know which is true.

So I will begin this letter in the hope that you will read it. If not immediately, then at some later time when you are ready. I need to tell you what happened, not minute-by-minute, but a broad sweep so you know the context of what I will write about later. How they pulled me apart, intruded into parts of my mind I thought were private. You have to understand this. I must speak with you.

You will remember that in the week before the arrests – or in your case, the shooting – we were nervous. We were uncertain because no one responded to our demonstration. Not a single letter of outrage to the paper, not a single report on TV or radio. Weird. And, so far as I know, only the things we wrote about in the lambda-group. We were puzzled, but we had not realised that it was a strategy. A strategy of silencing. How else to muzzle our protests?

And the night they came – what terror! I want to know what happened to you. Did they leave you for dead? They must have. Must have assumed like me that the bullet had killed you. But you, unlike me, have a close-knit family and they came as usual that morning to pass on some piece of family news that I would probably have called trivial. It saved your life. Your family, with its history of political subversion, is much better prepared than mine could ever be. They announced your death. What presence of mind. They had a death certificate to prove it. I know who would have written that. They buried you publicly, meanwhile you recuperated somewhere among friends. Your networks are more sophisticated that any other I know.

Who are you now Mercedes?

DESI

Is Mercedes still alive? After pulling a blank on the photos, I kept digging in the boxes and found some old rolls of film. I discovered someone at the film school and begged them to let me use the old equipment. "It's for my thesis," I said. They checked up on me and then made a time for me.

There is one film labelled 76. It's Super 8. It's a short film. I mean very short. Thirty seconds of Kate running along a path with a huge smile. It's in slow-mo.

I'm guessing this was an early experiment and Kate finished up with it because she's the subject of the film.

The other film is of two women. One is Kate. The other woman must be Mercedes. They are kissing. Two women kissing on film was not very likely back then. Mercedes turns to face the camera full on. It ends suddenly.

I ask to go back to the last few frames. I look carefully at Mercedes.

"Any chance of a print?" I ask.

I take the print home, hoping to compare it with the photo of the woman and girl outside Pablo's house.

It wasn't your mother who told me that you are alive, but your brother. He said he couldn't bear to watch me grieving over you, knowing that you lived. He told me some snippets, but he could not, he said, tell me where you were now and who you are. I am grateful to José for these crumbs, but it's not enough. To die, not to die – what is it? I have died and not died too. I have died over and over. I have died because I thought you had. I have died because of what they did to me. I have died because of things that were left unsaid. Because of what I didn't know. I have died and died and died.

DESI

This is hard to take. I don't get it either. Except maybe their different histories. For Kate, this is right now, her horror and she wants to be free. And she thinks Mercedes will make her free.

But Mercedes and her mother know that it's not over yet. That in Chile, it went on for years. They released people and rearrested them. Those who were released always led them to others. José is not at risk. He's more conventional, younger and he doesn't have quite the political passions Mercedes had.

I am so angry that you won't see me. So you nearly died! What of it?

DESI

I found him. José. It was a sort of accident and sort of planned. I've just met him in an obscure coffee shop at the wrong end of town. He looks a little like Mercedes, taller, thinner.

I took a few things with me. The photo still from the movie. I had to be sure it was really Mercedes. It is.

Then I pulled out the photo of Pablo's house.

"You have been doing your homework," he said when I said I thought it was Neruda's house in Valparaiso. He nodded.

"Is the girl Mercedes?"

He nodded again.

"The woman. Is it your mother?"

"No, my Aunt Carmen." He looked sad. "I never met her. But she was Mercedes' favourite aunt."

"After Neruda's death, everyone who knew him got scared. If they could brazenly kill him, then everyone was unsafe. Our family made plans. But they were naïve. Unpractised in the ways of terror."

"And?"

"It was hard to work out where to go. That's what my mother said. They found a way to get out, first by road north, then boat. She said they would work out where to go later."

"Why Australia?"

"It seemed safe. It was early 1975. A left government at the time. Days before they were ready to leave, Carmen was grabbed in the street. She'd been visiting some of her friends. Political friends. My mother says they were terrified. Who else would they take? Other family members? So they left, hoping Carmen

176

would be released and they'd be able to bring her to wherever they were."

"But she never came back?"

"No, never. She is one of the disappeared."

DESI

A scrap of newspaper. A tiny square that I almost missed because it was scrunched up in a corner of the last box. There is no date.

Mystery Killing

Brunswick. A woman was killed along with her dog two days ago. A second woman is missing. Police would like to speak to the missing woman about the dead woman. It is suspected that there may have been intruders. No names have yet been released.

I'm sorry about my outburst of yesterday. But I will try not to censor myself in this letter. I think it best if you know all of it, even the things you might not wish to know.

Do you remember my love of life? I have faint shreds of memory of the times we spent together when for no reason at all I laughed. We laughed. Out loud. Throwing back our heads in a kind of joy that now seems throwaway and careless. I wonder whether that was ever the case for you with your family's well-kept secrets. Was I just a light-hearted interlude in something bigger? Did you ever take me seriously? Well, now you could. I could parade before you my hurt, my visible scars and even those not easily seen. Is this what it takes to be considered real? Is it possible you despise me? I don't know where to go with this. I will wait for you to respond. How long? Uncertainty ravages me.

As you and your family know, trauma stays with you forever, just as grief does. It gets intertwined with who you are.

DESI

I had to ask José about Kate and Mercedes, but I didn't know how.

"I need to know this," I said. "For my research, but also for myself.

Did Kate and Mercedes meet again?"

He was silent. He ate a mouthful, paused again, swallowed some water.

"Yes. It took a long time."

José and I talked and talked and talked. They met overseas. One flew into Madrid. The other into Athens. They flew different airlines, different dates. Mercedes by now was used to her new identity. Her passport was in her new name. At the border Kate said she was visiting relatives. Then they spent a week in Rome, walking, talking, Kate showed Mercedes her favourite museum pieces and places. She took her to the Giardino dei Tarocchi in Umbria filled with giant tiled Tarot-inspired sculptures by Niki de Sainte Phalle. They joked about how they looked in the distorting mirrors. José told me there is a photo of them in that garden. After a week they parted again. Sometime in that week, they made an agreement. They assumed they would see one another again. If things changed enough, they would work out where to meet next. As far as I know, Kate died before things changed enough.

"And Mercedes?"

"I promised her I'd say nothing about now. Only the past."

After this conversation I couldn't sleep thinking about their relationship, the loss. For Kate it was the terrors of torture, the impossibility of ever recovering from that. For Mercedes too, a great loss. She lost all the friends she'd made in Australia and was locked in with her family. After all, she was officially dead. No matter how much you love them, you also need friends, lovers, companions of your own generation. All that had gone.

We meet at the Etruscan Museum. I don't see you at first because the person walking towards me does not walk like you. You had never shuffled and limped. And then I realise. I stand still, slowly we approach one another. If torture taught me one thing, it is patience.

We stand staring and then we hold one another. It is a long time before you speak.

"I so wish this hadn't happened."

I nod.

We walk around together looking at the old remains of the Etruscans. In a glass case is a beautiful sheep's head. Those Etruscans really knew their sheep. This one looks like a Border Leicester with its Roman nose.

As we are leaving, the most extraordinary exhibit I've ever seen, *Due uteri*, says the label. I look again. They are like conch shells. Next to the two, another two, are opened out. Each uterus resembles the rings of a tree trunk or even a spiral. We both laugh. We laugh and grab one another, grab ourselves with hysteria. We laugh until we cry. We leave the museum with tears on our cheeks. Tears of loss and love and more loss. All the days we have missed. The tears sweep away the anger we each have felt.

After our trip around the Museum, we head to the Villa Borghese via the back entrance and to their coffee shop. It's a bit of a walk, but that's what you do in Rome, even with one bung hip. We talk. I tell you some of what happened. I give you a few pages to read. You tuck them in your bag.

"And why are you limping?"

"The bullet hit me in the hip. I had help from a doctor in our community, and she did the best she could. But there were limits on what she could do. It's never properly healed. Sometimes people stand for me on the buses."

We are not staying in the same place, but nor are we far apart. It gives each of us the chance to take our time and take time out when needed. It's not easy. One night you come to my little room in Trastevere. And you stay. We hold one another as if we would never again let go. As light drifts in through the window, you reach out and hold my broken hand. The light carries the sharp heat of a hot Rome day.

José has been shopping for me. He might as well make himself useful while he's staying with me.

Kleio barks as José lets himself in through the front gate. She hasn't settled to him yet. He has some pisco to share. The sun is setting over the mountains all pink, like flamingos.

"You know that Kate's niece, Desi, has been on to me to answer questions," he begins. "Kate left her papers and her house to Desi."

"Well, not surprising, but what answers is she after?" Kleio stands up at the brusque sound of my voice and puts her head on my lap.

"Merci, I thought that it would be a good thing. You know that Kate wanted people to remember all the things you did together in that group."

"Sure, Kate and I went over this in Rome. We agreed we'd meet up again. But then she died on me a second time. It makes me angry all over again. As well as that, you know that I still can't afford to do anything public these days. Remember Carmen and all those others. They thought it was over, or that they'd slipped the net."

"Desi's worked some things out, and I do want to help her. She's a sweet kid. But wow, intense at times."

"Kate mentioned Desi a couple of times, but it was really in passing. She didn't tell me about the cancer diagnosis at the time and I expected we would meet again. Too late. This life is too hard. I can't see how I can help Desi, she'll have to help herself." I'm fondling Kleio's ears to keep her next to me.

"I was still so young and I barely knew what you were up to back in those days." José paused, "Why do you think they came after you?"

"Torturers don't need reasons. They just want to terrify you. Remember, those friends of Gertrude's in Germany who were raided by the police for attacking the repro tech and genetic engineering industry. Not only were they raided, they were charged with being 'terrorists'. It seems crazy, but I think the same stuff was going on here. They picked us out as a group that could get 'dangerous'. Their idea of it. None of us ever had any weapons other than our minds and our voices. Imagine if we were to do half the things so many men get up to. Gertrude's friends were never formally charged, but after that they were very scared. Every generation they pick on new groups. Call them terrorists, asocials, dangerous. The people at the top barely change. The people at the bottom are traumatised and re-traumatised. It's a form of social control."

"So can I tell her that?"

"Yeah, sure." Her voice shifted, "You can also tell her that I think Kate was incredibly brave. She told me some of what went on. And what happened just before they released her. I'll always love her for that. Her utter belief that I was dead has saved me. Tell her that my dogs are named for Kate in some way. She loved all those old stories and poems. And I loved that in her too."

DESI

Anna and I went to the Botanic Gardens today. Such a calm place. I said I had something to tell her. She hasn't read what I've written, although I have told her some things, it doesn't make sense unless you read it. We walked through the fern garden, so cool and green and moist, then up past the monkey puzzle tree with its spiralling branches, down to the prickly cactus garden and then to scones and coffee by the lake to the sounds of honking black swans.

"I heard from the examiners this morning," I say, my mouth filled with scone, jam and cream.

"And what did they say?"

I smile so wide that a bit of scone falls on the ground where it is instantly picked up by a fast-moving seagull.

"I did it," I splutter.

"So you'll be Dr Desi will you?"

"Not yet. As Kate would say, torture teaches you about patience. To be the missing girl Persephone, Penelope weaving and unweaving her texts, monstrous Echidna, grief-stricken Kyane, even the snakes in plain sight in mediaeval manuscripts."

Anna looks at me puzzled.

"Don't worry, you'll understand when you read my novel."

ACKNOWLEDGEMENTS

My first thanks go to the love of my life, Renate Klein who has endured conversations and difficult travels so that this book could be written. Renate has gone beyond what anyone in a relationship can expect: from living with the consequences of exploring trauma, travelling to sites where atrocities took place and always being my first reader and sternest critic. Also to all the lost dogs in my life, in particular to Freya who left far too soon. They teach us so much.

My thanks to artist and friend, Suzanne Bellamy, for the use of her art work on the cover and for inspiration and lesbian creativity over more than three decades.

The dedication to this book includes Christina, a Ugandan lesbian who in 2002 warned me about the dangers for lesbians in her country. Her warning was the catalyst for me to undertake research on the sorry subject of torture and why, when lesbians are tortured, there are no campaigns. Consuelo Rivera-Fuentes and Lynda Birke published one of the most important articles that exist on the torture of lesbians. They also welcomed us to their home and provided hospitality and more in England. Thank you to Consuelo for allowing me to ask questions. To X in Australia whose resilience and humour are an inspiration.

Estelle Disch deserves a special thanks for her knowledge of Buenos Aires and the history of Argentina's fall into dictatorship. Thanks to Estelle for her insight into Desi. Argentinian feminists have long been demonstrating and fighting for justice, among them Marta Fontenla and Magui Bellotti whose work and lives show just how persistent one has to be to resist and then effect change. To Luisa Valenzuela for a warm welcome and many masks.

Thanks to Juan Carlos Sáez for welcoming us to Chile, for Valparaiso and friendship. Also to Silvia Aguilera and Paulo Slachevsky for important conversations about the Pinochet regime.

Much gratitude to those who contributed in ways they might not know: Kaye Moseley, Suzanne Santoro, Robyn Arianrhod, Nelly Hearn, Vicky Black; to those who supported this book early: Juan Carlos Sáez, Colleen Higgs and Candida Lacey; and to readers who read drafts and gave insight to characters and plot so necessary to the novelist: Renate Klein, Estelle Disch, Doris Hermanns, Coleen Clare.

Thanks to all the women at Spinifex Press, Pauline Hopkins for insightful early edits and care with the text when I could no longer see the typos, Maralann Damiano for her great stamina, Helen Lobato for marketing nous and Caitlin Roper for social media. Also to Renate Klein wearing her Publisher's hat, Deb Snibson for her designer's eye and Helen Christie for text design and typesetting par excellance.

Thanks to the Australia Council for an Arts Project Grant that allowed me to finish this novel and complete the research. And to the Literarisches Colloquium Berlin (LCB) for hospitality at a critical writing time.

Lines quoted in the text by Gillian Hanscombe are from *Sybil: The Glide of Her Tongue*, Spinifex Press, 1992. Permission from the author.

Translations from Greek and Spanish are by Susan Hawthorne.

Parts of this manuscript were originally published in different forms on the *Project 365+1 Blog* during 2016 < http://

project365plus.blogspot.com.au/>. Thanks to Kit Kelen and Lizz Murphy for asking me to write a poem a day for a year and to all the participating poets who gave feedback on the work.

Other parts of the manuscript have been published in *Rabbit*, 2016; *Read These Lips,* 2008. <www.ReadTheseLips.com>; and the anthology *She Rises (Vol. 2)* edited by Helen Hye-Sook Hwang, Mary Anne Beavis and Nicole Shaw. Mago Books.

SOURCES

This book has been a work in progress since 2002. During the process of writing *Dark Matters* I have read countless books, personal testimonies as well as poetry and fiction. Writing a novel never happens in a straight line and much of my thinking owes a great deal to the work of lesbians around the world who, with enormous courage, have faced violence, humiliation – and indifference. *Dark Matters* could not have made the light of day without the following sources:

Munú Actis, Cristina Aldini, Liliana Gardella, Miriam Lewin and Elisa Tokar. 2006. *That Inferno: Conversations of Five Women Survivors of an Argentine Torture Camp*. Foreword by Tina Rosenberg. Translated by Gretta Siebentritt. Nashville: Vanderbilt University Press.

Rita Arditti. 1999. *Searching for Life: The Grandmothers af the Plaza de Mayo and the Disappeared Children of Argentina*. Berkeley: University of California Press.

Ariel Dorfman, Salvador Allende, Pablo Neruda, Joan Jara and Beatriz Allende. 2003. *Chile: The Other September 11*. Melbourne: Ocean Press.

David Kohut and Olga Vilella. 2010. *Historical Dictionary of the "Dirty Wars"*. Lanham: The Scarecrow Press.

Michael J. Lazzara (Ed.) 2011. *Luz Arce and Pinochet's Chile: Testimony in the Aftermath of State Violence*. Foreword by Jean Franco. New York: Palgrave Macmillan.

Consuelo Rivera-Fuentes and Lynda Birke. 2001. Talking with/in pain: reflections of bodies under torture. *Women's Studies International Forum*, Vol. 24, No. 6.

Elaine Scarry. 1985. *The Body in Pain: The Making and Unmaking of the World*. Oxford: Oxford University Press.

A number of other writers and books are mentioned in the text and I thank those authors for their courage, imagination and doggedness.

I began writing articles and presenting papers at conferences about lesbians who are tortured in 2003. The following are some published essays. Unpublished conference papers can be found at <http://susanspoliticalblog.blogspot.com.au/> or <https://jamescook.academia.edu/SusanHawthorne>

2005. Ancient Hatred and Its Contemporary Manifestations: The Torture of Lesbians. *The Journal of Hate Studies*. Vol. 4. 33–58. Online at <http://guweb2.gonzaga.edu/againsthate/Journal4/04AncientHatred.pdf>

2007. The Silences Between: Are Lesbians Irrelevant? *Journal of International Women's Studies*. Women's Bodies, Gender Analysis, and Feminist Politics at the Fórum Social Mundial. Vol 8. No 3 April, pp. 125–138. Online at <http://www.bridgew.edu/SoAS/jiws/April07/Hawthorne1.pdf>

2011. Are All Lesbians Sex Mad? The Fight for Lesbians' Human Rights <http://radicalhub.wordpress.com/2011/08/10/are-all-lesbians-sex-mad-the-fight-for-lesbians-human-rights/#more-2347>

Other Spinifex Press titles by Susan Hawthorne

THE FALLING WOMAN

Top Twenty Title, *Listener* Women's Book Festival
Year's Best Book List, *The Australian*

This book commands endless reflection, since it opens up the ontological question of being. Hawthorne's book haunts me, it won't let go. On the one hand, it journeys through an unexplored territory of mind that few apart from Dostoyevski dared look into… Let me first say that this is a perfectly structured piece of writing. Its form should help unravel the threads of signification, but we are not dealing here with the explicit, let alone the assertive, or blatant.

– Jasna Novakovic,
Australian Women's Book Review

ISBN 9781876756369

THE BUTTERFLY EFFECT

[The poems] are anything but typical; they are poignant postmodern echoes of a frustration with an intolerant past … I, for one, feel both enlightened and inspired for reading it through – three times. And I am still savouring the taste that lingers on my tongue.

– Heather Taylor Johnson,
Wet Ink

ISBN 9781876756567

COW

Shortlisted, Kenneth Slessor Poetry Prize,
NSW Premier's Literary Awards
Finalist, Audre Lorde Lesbian Poetry Prize

I recommend you lie in bed and read it to your lover, or pleasure yourself with it, mouth it, tongue it, and maybe as I did, circle its words and metaphors, annotate, indulge in marginalia, dally in thesauri and etymologies and listen and be encouraged to sing along.

– Sarah St Vincent Welch,
Rochford Street Review

ISBN 9781876756888

LUPA AND LAMB

Who'd have thought that erudition could be so exotic, erotic and dazzlingly entertaining? In this triumphantly inventive excursion into feminist revisionism, Hawthorne is fully mistress of language and genre as she brings her Roman women into view in the diverse roles – lover, poet, prostitute, martyr – and the sometimes dark fates that await them as living instances of she-wolf and lamb.

– Jennifer Strauss AM

ISBN 9781742199245

If you would like to know more about Spinifex Press,
write to us for a free catalogue, visit our website
or email us for further information.

Spinifex Press
PO Box 105
Mission Beach QLD 4852
Australia

www.spinifexpress.com.au
women@spinifexpress.com.au